Mysteries of the Body
and the Mind

Mysteries of the Body
and the Mind

stories

∞

JOHN TAYLOR

Story Line Press | Pasadena, CA

Mysteries of the Body and the Mind
Copyright © 1998, 2020 by John Taylor
All Rights Reserved

ISBN 978-1-58654-104-0 (softcover)
978-1-58654-105-7 (casebound)

The National Endowment for the Arts, the Los Angeles County Arts Commission, the Ahmanson Foundation, the Dwight Stuart Youth Fund, the Max Factor Family Foundation, the Pasadena Tournament of Roses Foundation, the Pasadena Arts & Culture Commission and the City of Pasadena Cultural Affairs Division, the City of Los Angeles Department of Cultural Affairs, the Audrey & Sydney Irmas Charitable Foundation, the Kinder Morgan Foundation, the Meta & George Rosenberg Foundation, the Allergan Foundation, the Riordan Foundation, Amazon Literary Partnership, and the Mara W. Breech Foundation partially support Red Hen Press.

Second Edition
Published by Story Line Press
an imprint of Red Hen Press
www.redhen.org

Acknowledgments

The author wishes to thank the editors of the following reviews, in which some of these stories first appeared: *Asylum, Bone & Flesh, Button, Color Wheel, Deklab Literary Arts Journal, Dream Scene Magazine, Flower, George and Mertie's Place, Grasslands Review, Habersham Review, The Illinois Review, The Paper Bag, The Pegasus Review, The Rambler, South Dakota Review.*

"Charlene," "Childhood Sweetheart" and "The Bon Ton" were published in the form of bilingual broadsides for the Festival de la Nouvelle in Saint-Quentin, France, in respectively 1991, 1992 and 1993. "Vassilis," "The Rented House," "A Daydream," "Thirst" and "The Food Stand" were grouped under the title *Apérceptions* and published as a broadside at the 1994 Festival de la Nouvelle.

"The Zerimiahs" was first published in a catalogue accompanying an exhibit of paintings by Christian Ziemert: *Ziemert, les delices de la contrainte*, Calais / Boulogne-sur-mer: Centre de Develeopment Culturel de Calais, 1986.

Contents

Quaestio mihi factus sum.
("I have become a question for myself.")
—Saint Augustine, *Confessions*

for Nature

Charlene

Charlene was never my girlfriend, but something attracted us to each other, we became confidants. Rachel never knew, nor did Rob. In that long, waxed, first-floor corridor of Franklin Junior High Charlene's locker stood next to mine, and in the morning before homeroom or during passing periods she would slip a word to me about her ups and downs.

"I'm still waiting for him to ask me."

"I'll try and find out what's going on."

Later than day, in gym class, I said to Rob:

"I've got the go-ahead."

The next morning, as we were hanging up our coats, Charlene held out her hand: Rob's identity bracelet was on her wrist.

I smiled, closed the locker door, spun the combination lock, strolled off to homeroom. I couldn't help feeling, for an instant, that I too was going steady with Charlene.

Charlene had the biggest tits in school and it perturbed me every time Rob and the other boys joked about them. They were impossible to miss, lying as they seemingly did atop the folders and books she cradled in front of her as she strolled down the hall. Rob hinted that he had fondled them, down in her basement, several times, and even suggested that he had gone somewhat further.

"Her parents leave us all alone down there," he boasted, breezy and sure of himself ever since Charlene had accepted to go steady with him. "And sometimes they even go out for the evening."

"Now tell us what her boobs are like," chided Charley Near, "so we can all get a hard-on."

"Do her nipples harden when you finger them?" interjected Jon Skidmore, a heavyset boy who by that time was tolerated by the others only because on such topics he had a great deal of information, being the only one who could read *Playboy* regularly, his father (an important administrator for the Des

Moines public school system), taking no other precaution than that of putting each monthly issue in the garbage can, with the other magazines.

Yet after Jon's precise questions Rob was never clear, contradicted himself.

"He's making it all up!" guffawed Dick, shoving Rob on the shoulder, nearly
knocking him down.

Doubts, however, remained.

Charlene came on strong, alluring, sensual. Her movements were warm
and graceful; her V-necked sweaters inevitably fit tight; she had a way of looking at you without blinking. When talking to me she would stand somehow
too close, as if to finger the buttons on my shirt. Once she said:

"You're the only boy I can talk to."

A tremor near nausea ran through me.

It was the same thing she said that day we danced. A few months had gone
by; it was the spring semester; the Student Council elections had been held; I
had become Vice President; Charlene, Social Coordinator.

We're supposed to go to East High next Tuesday for an all-city meeting,"
she announced one morning. "Mr. Bench said he'd drive. Bill won't be able to
go. So you're in charge. You'd make a better president, anyway."

Bill, who was also one of Charlene's former boyfriends, was the President
of our Student Council.

After the meeting there was a dance.

"Come on," she said, dragging me to the dance floor, "show me what you
can do."

I couldn't do much, but Charlene held on for us both, tightly, and put her
head on my shoulder. I immediately felt embarrassed, because of Rachel, at
the same time acquiesced in everything Charlene asked me to do. She took
the lead. In a while I relaxed. Indeed, in a while, I felt in her arms secure about
myself and the entire world.

"You're the only boy I can talk to," she whispered into my ear.

We danced to three or four songs, talking no longer. Peter, Paul & Mary
sang, then The Dave Clark Five. Finally Mr. Bench, with a worldly smile, told
us we had to leave. The school year wound to a close; the next year Charlene
and I went to different high schools. Once or twice I saw her at basketball
games. Cooney, who took drawing lessons with her at the Art Center, where
she was considered the most gifted student in recent history, mentioned her
occasionally. Came college. I never saw Charlene again.

With Rachel, I should add, things came to a conclusion as well—a temporary conclusion.

Years later, back from Europe, I learned from my mother that Charlene had married one of the All-American boys in town—a straight-A student, an All-State basketball player. I of course know Gordon very well. He was a year older than I was; in Little League we had often played against each other; he lived only a few streets away. He was a pretentious ass.

It was none other than Gordon whom my mother had often held up to me as a model—not his unbearable cockiness as a star athlete and scholar, but rather his truly impressive accomplishments, doubted by none. And above all, his drive "to be the very best at whatever he did," as my mother put it. It is alas too late to explain to her that I am now more or less, no, increasingly sure that if I had actually followed Gordon down his glorious path—done this or that, that or this, the things expected of boys, of young men, like I was back then—then "Yes, Mom, I agree, my life today would be easier, much easier, but I would not be myself!"

So Gordon and Charlene had immediately had a child. Gordon began practicing in the office of one of the high-society dentists. A second child came. But gossip spread that Charlene was running around. Some claimed the second child was not Gordon's. Black hair? Where was the fair complexion of its parents? Various theories were expounded: no one really knew Mendel's Laws. At last was announced the divorce. Gordon moved to Minneapolis, leaving Charlene in Des Moines with the two children.

"Thank goodness Dr. Fletcher was able to get Gordon into an excellent practice up there," added my mother. "They say he's getting his life back together."

"So what's Charlene doing now?" I inquired. "Has she continued painting?"

As always when hearing such stories, I imagined myself coming to her rescue. Her extraordinary landscapes, Iowa farmland as no one had ever depicted it—not the permanence of beloved countryside, but rather the fragility, the ephemerality, of plowed soil, languorous streams, oak trees, humid air, hazy light. Iowa as I too felt it.

"Well, they say . . ."

We ended up in an argument. When we arrived home we separated. I went upstairs. We didn't speak to each other for the rest of the evening.

∞

Sometimes in the middle of the night, when awakened by a nightmare or a noise, I cannot fall back to sleep at all. I try to stay as calm as I can, remembering a scientific article which I once read and which proved that even incurable insomniacs actually sleep more than they claim to do. Thus I remember the article and instead of tossing and turning, I very quietly pull back the covers of our bed, bring my legs around and down to the floor, search for my espadrilles with my toes, slip into them, reach for the book atop the pile alongside the bed, rise, tiptoe out of the room. Françoise knows what I am up to, turns over, does not worry, falls back to sleep.

Our living-room couch, how well I know it. (As the Greek poet C. P. Cavafy might have said.)

Françoise has been saying recently that we should get rid of that couch, buy a real one, a comfortable one, with a pull-out bed for visiting friends.

And I can't help but agree. The brown corduroy fabric covering is worn, has stretched in unsightly ways, bunches up in the middle. After all, it is a makeshift couch, put together with cushions.

Our living-room couch, how well I know it.

It was made by neighbors of ours, Brazilians, who left it behind, the day they left Paris for good. Our entryway mirror also comes from that family that we liked, spent time with, then never heard from again.

Now we too have left Paris, for the provinces.

Our living-room couch, how well I know it.

For a long time during those sleepless night, I simply lie on the couch, listening to the occasional passing car, thinking about the past and the future, the lamp on, the book beside me on the floor. At such an hour, the twists and turns of my life always seem so mysterious. How did I, from Des Moines, from Franklin Junior High, end up all the way over here?

I remember many things, many events, many people.

For example, Charlene.

And whenever I think about Charlene for a while, she always says, at the end, at this strange hour of the night:

"That was nice."

That I rescued her? (But I did not.) That I danced with her and tried to do my best? (She probably said something like that.) That I remembered her?

Yes, I remember Charlene from time to time.

A car passes, far away, on the avenue Pasteur.

Is the car coming to town? Back to town? Leaving? Leaving for good?

I listen for the answer. The distant sound of the engine and of the wheels on the wet pavement fades to silence. The car heads in a direction I cannot determine.

I imagine the night. The night is just outside the living-room window.

I try to think of nothing now, knowing there is no definite answer, anyway.

Mme Singer

Sometimes I switch on the lamp and start thinking about Mme Singer in her one-room apartment full of old furniture and her son's paintings. She has invited us to tea. Her hand trembles as she lifts the porcelain cup to her lips. She speaks about architecture and her fears of mountain climbing, ever in relation to her son, then about her husband's bankruptcy, his death. I realize that none of her former problems has been solved: friends still live too far away to call on her; crossing the busy avenue remains perilous—the gusts of wind, the pushing crowds! On her bedside table lies a novel written by one of the difficult contemporary authors.

"My son lent it to me," she remarks.

"What was her first name?" asks Françoise.

"I don't remember," I reply.

"Was it Lydia?"

"Maybe that was it."

"It started with an "L." It as a rare name, aristocratic."

"Liana?"

We knew her very little: an elevator door held open; an errant run. When she learned from Françoise that my mother had died, she spoke to me in the corridor. That evening we invited her to dinner and Françoise made an onion tart. But it was precisely onions that the doctor had proscribed.

"I'll just have a sliver," she said, taking a dainty bite, leaving the rest on her plate.

("*Mais non*, it wasn't the onions, it was the salt! And she said I made the best chocolate cake in Europe!")

She spoke about her cures at Vichy. Over the years she had made acquaintances there, with one lady in particular. Every August, every afternoon, they would sit in the lobby of the hotel, chatting about their long-deceased husbands, about burglaries, murders, also about the metro and the buses.

"Then we would read our magazines," she explained.

Mme Singer read the architectural magazines that her son would bring her and subscribed to *La Revue des Deux Mondes*, a once-influential literary journal. When the Socialists came into power she would ask me to buy, not only *Le Figaro*, but also *Le Matin*; and from the *magasin arabe* on the rue George-Eastman, a bottle of Bordeaux and several bars of chocolate. Her lipstick was always bright red, rather garish.

From these and other details we imagined a former life of happiness, comfort, culture, followed by sudden tragedy. After her husband's death she had moved from the 16th to the 13th arrondissement and rented a studio in one of the high-rise apartment buildings near the place d'Italie. We never learned how and when Mme Singer had arrived in France, from Rumania.

"Back then, during our first years here"—but did she mean before or after the Second World War?—"my husband knew all the best little shops. From his rounds he would bring back coffee, tarama, poppy-seed cakes, sometimes a special loaf of bread, sometimes the best Greek olives, a Georgian wine...."

He seemed to have been a sales representative and, from all appearances, she had loved him very much.

She was our neighbor for several years. But we knew her very little, as I said.

A few days after she died at the hospital, her daughter-in-law knocked on our door.

"Mme Singer wanted you to have something of hers," she explained. "My husband and I thought of giving you the choice of a chest of drawers or this lamp."

She held out a blue vase with a floral design, crowned by a dingy beige lampshade. In her other hand she was holding the plug and electric cord.

I have always avoided dwelling over such choices and, in much the same way that from several mementoes laid out on the bed by my father I picked up my mother's blue purse, I said:

"Well, the lamp, I suppose."

The daughter-in-law handed me the lamp, thanked me again for having been such a good neighbor, said good-bye, then walked off towards the elevator. I went into the living room, propped the lamp up against the cushions of the couch. I looked at it for a while, then went back into the other room, sat down at my desk.

I stopped feeling uneasy only when Françoise returned, full of news and good cheer, a few minutes before one o'clock, earlier than usual: the driver of the bus that she usually just missed had let her in at the stoplight.

The Hiding Place

For months we had known that the tiny rosewood box had perhaps been lost during the moving.

But that evening when we spoke about it again, and even got up and looked here and there—in that never-opened suitcase full of old sheets; behind the books, on all the shelves; inside the plastic tabourets where long ago the box had been hid—I suddenly felt ashamed. My mother's ring had been in the box; I had forgotten.

"I don't even remember what it looked like."

"You know, a thin gold band, red and white jewels."

"Were they real jewels?"

"No."

"I see the ring now. My mother always wore jewelry like that at the end."

I pictured the ring on my mother's finger: her puffy white skin, the liverish blotches that come with age—she had a name for them . . . Those liverish blotches that I now have, myself.

The next morning Françoise remembered, found the box in her old navy-blue handbag. It was the handbag that she had carried when we first met: large, rather oblong; the leather had worn well; only one of the handles would need to be re-sewn.

I remarked:

"I remember how you arranged your folders in that handbag, before heading to your classes at Asnières."

We examined the rings (there were several others), then put them back into the box. Then put the box back into the handbag. And the handbag back into the closet.

A Daydream

I daydreamt I was standing alongside a teacher whom I had feared long ago. I turned my head to the right. Miss Hamilton stood there silently, without moving, her arms at her sides. She was wearing, as was to be expected, a faded sack dress depicting a myriad of tiny flowers. Her hair was cropped short, like a boy's.

I looked at her for quite some time. She now seemed harmless, even vulnerable, and in addition (I soon realized) she was made of wax.

"I have the upper hand," I thought.

I was no longer standing, but instead rising from my seat in the classroom. I was invisible. Taking my books under my arm, I had decided to tiptoe out of the room. My classmates burst out in uncontrollable laughter once my two books started floating in front of their eyes.

"What should I do now?" I wanted to ask Rex, my best friend that year, who was talented at making us laugh. "What should I do for an encore?"

With this question my daydream faded, leaving me disappointed that, as usual, I had failed to be a leader, failed (literally) to rise to the occasion. The wind was rustling the wooden shutters, the sunlight was glaring off the building next door. I wondered (daydreaming again) if Miss Hamilton was going to punish me for all the antics that I had performed while invisible.

But what antics had I performed? I had not really done anything except stand there, invisible, holding my books. It was my classmates who had laughed hysterically, causing Miss Thorne, the principal, to come from her office. Was I really guilty? If I was guilty, wasn't Miss Hamilton just as guilty? It was because of her that I had wanted to slip out of the room—unseen, unheard. It was because of her that I had become invisible. I had desired to do an encore, that is true, but I had only thought of asking Rex for advice on how to do one. The books that I had taken from my desk were my own.

No conclusions seemed to follow from these thoughts, and in a moment I began feeling sorry—not for Miss Hamilton—but rather that our respective paths had crossed on earth. It would have been better, much better, had we never met. I imagined what the world would have been like, had I been born in Burma. As far as Miss Hamilton and I are concerned, it would have been a much better world.

The thought of being born and raised in Burma made me think of temples, which made me think of fire. Suddenly (still daydreaming) I was holding a candle, and there was nothing but night all around us: me and the enormous wax statue of Miss Hamilton.

Musette Disappears

I always imagine Musette wearing her white dress and her Easter bonnet with the pink ribbon. She is standing at the entryway to the church; the service is over; Father Kemble is shaking her parents' hands; Musette has turned her head and is gazing absently at something beyond the cars parked on Urbandale Avenue. And then Father Kemble bends down and takes her tiny gloved hand, somewhat startling her. She smiles, nods her head, squinting into the sun.

Musette disappears.

Back then her parents would lead her past us—my mother and father chatting with the family who lived in Johnston—Musette unaware (as far as I could tell) of my presence.

Skipping past me, looking down at her feet.

I would watch her skip across the parking lot; stand next to her parents' long, waxed, blue Impala; get in.

Musette disappears.

Musette always disappears. I can return at will to these brief moments of my past, of Musette's past, but back then didn't I already know somehow—I think I did—that this radiant presence come into my life was destined to be transient, to reappear only to disappear?

Blacky's Story

Blacky was the dachshund puppy that we went all the way out to West Des Moines to buy one Saturday morning just after Christmas. I had never been in that part of the city before, but like those in our neighborhood the streets were quiet and lined with towering elm trees.

Yet something was not quite the same; I couldn't really determine what.

In a moment we found the house number, parked the car, got out, walked up the driveway. We knocked on the front door. A lady appeared, told us to go around to the side of the house.

There an aluminum door opened, to the outside; we crossed the threshold; a second door was already open, to the inside. We stood on the landing for a moment. Then the lady reappeared, hurriedly, out of breath, as if between her opening the second door and our entering the house she had run to the kitchen to take a pot off the stove or hang up the phone. She smiled, ushered us down the carpeted stairs into the basement. In a corner, in a large wooden box, four tiny puppies were playing, fighting, scrambling up and over each other. Ann immediately chose the black one of the bunch.

The lady handed our father the pedigree. I strained to get a look as he examined it—a sheet of stiff paper, oblong, rather like a piece of parchment. There were countless rectangles, alongside several of which red or blue marks, shaped like tiny keyholes, could be seen.

"Those are the champions," explained the lady when I touched one of the marks with my finger. "Your dog is a pure-blooded descendent of prizewinners."

"May we keep the pedigree?" asked our father.

I had learned about pedigrees only that morning. Ann had read the want ad aloud: "pedigree" was the magic word that had changed our mother's mind. She had had two dogs as a child, both poisoned by a neighbor; it was a story she often told. But every time we (especially Ann) asked about getting a dog she looked away, bit her lower lip, changed the subject. I am now sure that in our mother's mind a pedigree guaranteed a clean dog, one that wouldn't want to sleep in her bed, might not even bark or go into heat.

"Blacky," as we quickly and unanimously agreed to name him, was a "boy."

We must then have stopped at a pet shop and bought all the necessary equipment. All I remember happening next on that special day was Blacky struggling against his chain in the back yard. . . . I am getting ahead of myself: Blacky was a puppy when we bought him; he must have struggled against that chain several weeks, perhaps several months later. For the time being, Blacky was confined to the house, and soon to the kitchen.

Exactly how soon I am not sure, but I remember all of us driving to Iltis Lumber Company, having a sheet of Masonite cut to measure. There was a open passageway between the living room and the kitchen; the sheet of Masonite was going to keep Blacky "out of trouble," as our mother put it. The two other passages to or from our small kitchen—between the kitchen and the den, between the kitchen and the back porch—could be closed off with doors.

As always, our father's calculations were precise. The sheet of Masonite was held perfectly in check once we had slid one end several inches into the space between the refrigerator and the wall. We then pushed the refrigerator even closer to the wall.

The sheet of Masonite was well over two feet high. Our parents could step over it; I could step over it; but Ann and Joan could not. From the kitchen they would take the long way around to the living room, via the den. Taking great precautions, constantly pleading with Blacky to back up, they would ever so slowly turn the knob of the den door, keeping Blacky at bay with one foot, eventually squeezing their way through.

Sometimes Ann or Joan rode the sheet of Masonite like a horse, Blacky yapping and biting at the stockinged foot on the kitchen side of the barrier . . . until one afternoon when, Ann having cried "giddy up" and veered to the right, the whole system collapsed.

I had been sitting at the kitchen table.

The sheet of Masonite warped slowly, very slowly, Ann leaning farther and farther away from me, everything taking place as if in slow motion—until the sheet snapped, hurtling her to the ground. Her laughter burst into the air. Blacky escaped, leaping over her, racing and tearing up and down and all over the house until I finally managed to tackle him in the den. In the middle of the confusion he had found the time to hop up on the living-room sofa and lay a turd. Fortunately, even before we got Blacky, our mother always kept the satiny white upholstering of the living-room furniture covered with old sheets.

After everything had settled down once again, with Blacky locked outside on the back porch despite the winter temperatures, our mother called our father at his office so that he would stop at Iltis's for a new sheet of Masonite. Ann whispered to me:

"I think that Mom's really tense about Blacky."

We came to use the expression more and more often.

Blacky enjoyed some pleasure with us, he also knew pain. About the time we got him, Bernadette, the youngest and most vicious of the notorious Cellinis, had stopped turning on neighbors' water faucets and then leaving—a stunt she had learned from Jimmy, her brother, by this time in reform school—and instead had started torturing every dog she could get her hands on. Bernadette tortured Blacky several times, whipping, jabbing, gouging, hampering him with those makeshift weapons with which all five Cellini children were armed. Soon we understood that we could not leave Blacky alone even for as long as it took to run inside for a glass of lemonade. When we returned, Bernadette would be bent over him, one of her hands muffling his snout, the other trying to pull a hind leg out of its socket. I would run after her, chasing her from our property, but turn back as soon I had reached he edge of 48th Street. Jimmy might just that day have returned home on parole.

The Zerimiah boys also tortured Blacky—once, horribly.

What Blacky liked most of all was escaping from his backyard chain. We arranged the escapes, of course, sitting down with Blacky in the grass, talking to Blacky, petting Blacky, fingering the button that would unhook the chain, tempted to unhook Blacky but knowing that we shouldn't, looking around to see if our mother was watching, tempted even more, looking around again, no mother in sight, finally unhooking Blacky and screaming that Blacky had broken loose!

Off Blacky would run, streaking across the patio, down the driveway, always heading left across Nana's front lawn, across the Farny's lawn, onwards to Snyder Drive. Alerted by our cries, the children playing outside—Jeannie, Peter, Diana, Little Leonard, not to forget Bernadette and the Zerimiah boys—would join us in the chase, to the left down Snyder Drive, past 48th Street Place, towards 49th Street and the Methodist Church. Strangely, instead of crossing the street and heading across the field next to the church, Blacky would invariably turn left (once again) at 49th Street, churn up the sidewalk past my drum teacher's house, past Crazy Ken's house, children from that neighborhood joining in, Crazy Ken joining in as well, Blacky beginning to tire in the meantime, his tiny legs not being able to bear much longer his heavy, oblong body.

Blacky stopping to catch his breath.

Panting.

Panting.

Dodging a tackle by streaking off at the last instant.

Not being able to streak off a second or third time.

One of us would catch him and Blacky would be carried back to the house—in triumph.

I do not remember Blacky eating dog food from a dish or lapping water from a bowl, though he must have been fed that way. On the back porch? I doubt that we fed him scraps from the table.

Blacky's dog collar, with two, perhaps three or four, dangling tags. At least one was silver, another one blue.

The veterinarian to whom we took Blacky once (twice?) for shots. His office was located on Hickman Road, not far from the house that had a cage in the front yard—with a monkey inside.

∞

Blacky's long, silky ears: the curious folds of skin inside his ears. Blacky's padded paws, the desire, while I was petting him, to lift one of his paws and touch that rough padding.

∞

Blacky's penis, the 30°, perhaps 20° angle between it and his belly.

∞

A photo that I could try to find—it is surely in that box of family pictures, which lies underneath other boxes in our storage room. The photo depicts Ann and Blacky—at Christmas? Ann is holding Blacky upright, hugging him around the neck. Blacky's eyes gleam, reflecting the flash of the camera.

∞

A much more recent photograph, probably in the same box. This time Ann is pictured with her dog Jupiter. She had won a prize in a drawing, which enabled her to have her picture taken, free, by a professional photographer. Grrr, her cat, is also in the picture. Jupiter died last year.

∞

As I write this, the dog on the fourth-floor balcony of the apartment building on the other side of the rue de Belgique. The dog is taking in the morning sun, on a particularly cold March morning.

∞

Blacky's backyard chain, held in place by a long steel spike driven into the ground. Our father probably borrowed a mallet from Mr. Manson to drive the spike into the ground.

∞

Did we have a leash for Blacky? Did we ever take Blacky for a walk?

∞

One day our mother took us downtown to Younkers; she bought us each quite a few things: new shoes, books, clothes for Ann and Joan, even white chocolate; when we came home our father was there; where was Blacky?

He had been taken "to a farm."

Our parents promised that "we could go and see him soon."

"But first we should let Blacky get used to his new owners," explained our father.

"Where's the farm?" asked Ann.

"The farm is about 20 miles out of town."

"I want to go right now," said Ann.

Tears were welling in her eyes.

Somehow our father calmed Ann down; we didn't go to see Black that day; nor the next day.

Nor the day after that.

∞

In the years that followed, if our pain (and especially Ann's) did not really disappear, asking our mother (but usually our father) to take us "to see Blacky" became a family joke. One of those family jokes which conceal much bitterness, but which are told in families for years—for that very reason. Usually the subject would come up at dinnertime, prompted by some distant allusion: someone else's dog, the color "black," the word "farm." "Take us to see Blacky!" we would sob, our mother not saying a word, our father defending himself:

"Hey, come on, get off my back!"

∞

Years later Joan announced her engagement to Randy. I decided to fly back to the States for the wedding. Françoise and I looked all over Angers for a present; finally we found a Japanese bowl in the raku style. While in the gift shop Françoise suggested that I take something to Ann as well.

"You see each other so seldom," she said.

We looked at all sorts of other oriental items; we kept telling the shop owner that this time we wanted something French.

Finally he opened a box and, one by one, took out an assortment of small hyperrealist statues—of dogs. He set them out on his desk. We laughed, they were pretty kitschy; then I recognized Blacky.

"Blacky was just like this," I remarked, ignoring the shop owner, picking up one of the statues, handing it to Françoise.

We bought it and had the man wrap it up.

After dinner, in Des Moines, Ann and Joan unwrapped their presents. When Ann opened hers, we all broke out in imitation sobs, begging our father to take us to see Blacky. He took it very badly, making a nasty remark about how we had never understood who, of him and our mother, was to blame.

Then he got up and left the room.

I went after him, caught up with him in his study, put my hand on his shoulder.

"Don't take a joke so hard, Dad. We all know that Mom was the guilty one."

"But even if Mom was the main culprit," retorted Ann, many more years later, when Françoise and I were visiting her in Nashville, "Dad could have put his foot down and said no. I'm still pissed off about the whole thing."

I noticed the statue of Blacky, somewhat dusty, sitting on Ann's desk, next to her phone and answering machine. We went out for tacos.

And that is Blacky's story, as far as I can tell it.

The O'Connell Sisters

By now the O'Connell Sisters are surely dead. Back then they were at least sixty, and how many times didn't we hope and pray they were kicking off, their Venetian blinds drawn, doctors coming and going, Tobey up from his store delivering groceries, the brother from Omaha arriving on Thursday? . . .

Then he would come out of the house, look around, finger the handle of the car door, look around again, finally get in, rev the engine, slowly back down the driveway.

A few more days would pass.

By the next weekend the spinster twins would reappear, take up their usual positions on the front porch, Helen in the left lawn chair, Ruth in the right, restored fully to vim and malevolence, wearing their wide-brimmed straw sunbonnets, gripping each a flyswatter. Until nightfall they would once again watch over their front lawn, not too far from which we were forced to play, in the street, the Methodist Church having expanded over our baseball field, the vacant lot at the corner of 48th Street Place and Snyder Drive having finally been bought and fenced off, the other nearby streets being either too busy or lined with parked cars. If a baseball or football or balsawood glider came to rest at but the corner of their property, it was gone.

"We'll see about that," Ruth would say, smiling, while Helen tiptoed across the lawn and picked up the ball. When she returned she too would say, smiling:

"We'll see about that . . . tomorrow."

But when the next morning several of us would knock on their door, no one would answer.

We soon got our fathers involved, but none of them, not even the amiable Mr. Matthews, Nancy's father, ever recovered anything. When my home-made kite got tangled in their linden tree, my father took a deep breath, headed their way, only to return a half-hour later with a strained look on his face:

"I'll make you another one," he promised.

"They know their law," was Mr. Meert's explanation. "We can't do a thing."

We turned to Mr. Manson, always riled up about something, anyway.

But he, too, came back sullen and empty-handed.

We kids then declared war on the O'Connell sisters and they, in retaliation, bought two small dogs. Whenever a ball did land on their property, it became a race to see who would get there first, we or the O'Connell sisters, shrieking, and their sicced dogs. Sometimes the police were called out; the same heavyset officer with traces of talcum powder on his cheeks would drive up in his cherry-top, tell us to play further on. But there was no further on. Past Nancy's, the Harris's had bordered their lawn, the only flat one in the neighborhood, with marigolds. All that was left to us was the street, the section running from Nancy's, past Steve's, to the O'Connell sisters' one-story house.

We took revenge on the O'Connell sisters by ringing their doorbell and running away, by phoning and breathing heavily or whispering dirty words, even at times by flinging eggs or ripe tomatoes or mudballs against their house. But afterwards our parents always made us clean up the mess ourselves.

"Listen, Johnny," my mother would say, her long fingernails digging into my shoulder blades, "you do what is right. They'll suffer for how they treat people."

But suffer where? But suffer when? When Steve and I knocked out their kitchen window with slingshots, we had to pay for the new pane of glass out of our allowances. Why didn't Ruth and Helen O'Connell have to pay for the baseballs and footballs and Frisbees that they seized and never returned?

Then, almost overnight, we grew up. We played such games less often. Junior high had intervened, then high school. My closest friends were no longer from the neighborhood; they lived a long way away, one group of them in Windsor Heights, a second group in the new residential area around the new high school. My parents, too, decided to leave the neighborhood and started talking about looking for a house.

One evening two years later, just before we moved into the house which (as it turned out) we had had built in the same new residential area around the new high school, I ran into Nancy at Ruth and Ernie's. Nancy and I talked, passed through Ruth and Ernie's hedge, continued talking in her backyard. A horde of children was about, her cousins I think. We decided to show them how to play Annie Over.

Steve appeared, from the basement bedroom in which he was spending more and more of his time. He stood in his backyard, I in Nancy's. We started throwing the tennis ball back and forth over Nancy's garage. Then for some reason I wound up and purposely threw the ball not only over Nancy's garage, but also over Steve's—into the O'Connell sisters' backyard. The children ran that way, towards the fence separating Steve's backyard from the O'Connell sisters' property. Laughing, we kept them from touching it. We told them it was electrified.

Someone asked: "Well, what do we do now?"

No longer fearing the O'Connell sisters, I decided to see what would happen.

I walked between the two houses, turned at the sidewalk, turned again at their driveway, walked up the driveway to their front door. As I knocked, the door opened, as if they were expecting me. I started to speak, but Ruth interrupted. She put her finger to her lips. She said I could fetch the tennis ball, then closed the door.

I must have walked slowly around their house to their backyard. Their backyard gate must have been un-padlocked. I must have pushed the gate. For all I remember is stooping to pick up the ball from the grass, rising, turning, starting to head back, then stopping and standing there motionless and uneasy, watching the O'Connell sisters watching me.

The Zerimiahs

That we eventually got entangled in a lawsuit with Mr. Zerimiah because of an incident involving a splinter did not surprise my mother who, the first time she saw him, declared:

"That man means trouble."

She was standing by the front window. I ran over to her.

Sitting in front of the house where Dave had lived, the new neighbor, burly and bare-chested, was drinking beer. When he stood to remove another box from the station wagon, we saw he was wearing a pair of gym shorts so tight they looked like underpants. His belly was enormous. The sweat on his burned skin glistened in the afternoon sun.

The man tugged a cardboard box out the back end and onto the tailgate, hefted it onto his belly, then carried it in a comic, half-strutting, half-staggering manner over to the front steps. There the box plummeted down. Drunkenness, also fatigue, a sort of drowsy hilarity, had manifestly overcome him. He sought the lawn chair with his hand, plopped himself down, fumbled in the grass for another can, popped it open. He laughed out loud. My mother moved behind the curtain—utterly disgusted.

That same day we learned that Mr. Zerimiah—it was Nana who told us his name—had bought the building that housed Kempf Realty, on Beaver Avenue, and turned it into a spacious garden, hardware, and lumber store.

A week later my father and I went to see what Mr. Zerimiah was like.

He was standing behind the cash register when we walked in—an obese man of average height, with short hair, a large forehead, a double chin, a thin moustache above a fleshy upper lip. What from the window had seemed an eye patch was turned out to be a port-wine stain around his right eye. Mr. Zerimiah did not recognize us. He was stirring something in a bucket, a sort of liquid conglomerate made up of sand, cement, and pebbles.

"We're neighbors," announced my father, dropping a twenty-pound bag of peat on the counter and laying a pinewood board alongside. "We live across the street."

Mr. Zerimiah grunted an acknowledgment, shook my father's hand, started punching the cash register. With his eye he measured the thickness of the board.

"That one goes for $1.89," he muttered, seemingly to himself.

My father slid the board in our direction, tucked it under his arm; suddenly a splinter lodged in his palm.

"Dammit!" he cried, setting the board back down, fluttering his hand in pain.

But it was not the splinter that lead to the lawsuit.

Mr. Zerimiah had two sons, Jimmy and Danny, the former younger, the latter older than I was. One day I finally mustered the courage to introduce myself to them.

"What are you guys doing?" I asked, noticing in Danny's hand several small firecrackers.

"We're playing a game called 'massacre,'" answered Jimmy. "Watch."

His brother bent down, stuck one of the firecrackers into the opening of an anthill. But before he could light it I was gone. I was afraid of firecrackers; besides, my mother was surely watching.

There were other such stores in Des Moines. There were other playmates in the neighborhood. Had the splinter incident not intervened, perhaps we would have gone on living in peace with the Zerimiahs for years—having not the slightest thing to do with them, which is what living in peace is usually all about. But one day Blacky broke loose from his stake and, dragging his long chain behind, trotted over into the Zerimiah's front yard. At just that moment Jimmy and Danny were playing a new game there, sticking splinters of wood into their sister Diana's stuffed ragamuffin doll.

Mr. Pierre

What was his name? Everybody called him by his last name, but it was one of those last names that are actually first names, something French, something like Mr. Pierre. He lived just north of town, not far from the Firestone plant, along the Interstate. Why my mother went there to have her hair styled I never could understand. Many of her friends went too. Mr. Pierre gambled heavily; while cutting hair he whispered constantly into the telephone receiver, kept in place between his jaw and shoulder; they said his breath smelled of alcohol; in the waiting room of his beauty parlor (a part of his house) golf and hunting magazines and unemptied ashtrays lay about on a coffee table covered with heel marks and water stains.

"There are even *Playboy* magazines," added my mother.

"I can't believe that you of all people go there," I remarked.

"But he cuts hair so well and he's so cheap."

My mother's values vanished whenever she was talking about Mr. Pierre.

"Mr. Pierre—when you get to know him—is a wonderful human being. He's just a little . . . risqué."

I was quite a golfer back then and my mother was always trying to organize a match between me and Mr. Pierre.

"But he doesn't want to play with you," she would add. "He says you might get corrupted."

"Corrupted?"

"Mr. Pierre says he can't play golf without betting."

"Then we won't play."

"I'll try to work something out."

I did eventually play golf with Mr. Pierre, but it was not my mother who organized the match. We met at a weekend tournament sponsored by the town of Ankeny. I did not know who Mr. Pierre was, but our names were drawn for the same foursome; as we were introducing ourselves, he said:

"Jesus, you're Jan's kid."

He shook my hand vigorously, as if we were long-lost friends, then walked me towards the clubhouse.

"I'll probably get a little betting game going with the other two," he said, putting his arm around my shoulder, gripping it. "But don't let them talk you into joining. God, it's great to meet you!"

The betting game did get going and whenever he could, winking me into complicity, Mr. Pierre cheated. Winter rules were no longer in effect, so the ball had to be taken as it lay; but Mr. Pierre, dangling his four-iron behind his leg and feigning to watch the others, always managed to set the ball up on a tuft of grass. In the rough, balls which from the tee had seemed surely lost appeared, a little farther than expected, out of danger. And on a particularly tough three-wood shot over a creek all of us had seen the splash. Mr. Pierre went on ahead. The rules in force stipulated that, with a two-stroke penalty, the next shot would have to be taken on the near side of the creek. But when we caught up with him, we found him standing in the reeds on the far bank.

"It must have bounced," he remarked with such authority and experience in his voice that everyone was convinced.

It is true, they sometimes bounced. It is also true that through a hole in their pocket golfers could drop a new ball down their pantleg.

I do not know how much money Mr. Pierre won that day. I saw no money changing hands. But it may have been a considerable amount. I later learned from D. J. that Mr. Pierre sometimes played at Waveland in the afternoon with those notorious golfers, all of Italian origin, who on a single hole would bet up to a thousand dollars.

"But where does he get the money?" I asked. "He's my mother's hairdresser."

"Come out and see for yourself," he replied.

I met D. J. after school at Waveland. Mr. Pierre was in the clubhouse, drinking.

"How's life?" he asked when I came over to his table.

But he was looking past me, his eyes tired, bloodshot, the skin on his face waxy, lifeless. When two hours later D. J. and I returned to the clubhouse Mr. Pierre was still in the bar, his head now down on the table.

That was the last time I saw Mr. Pierre. From my mother I learned that he had married off his only daughter, that he had bought a boat, then a cabin at Clear Lake, that his liver had been giving him fits. He eventually went through a detoxification program. It was apparently that which changed him.

The next thing they knew he had started up a campaign to install wheelchair ramps in front of public buildings.

"I admit," explained my mother, "that he doesn't make us laugh as much as he used to. All he talks about now is what can be done for the handicapped."

"But why the handicapped?" I asked. "Is his daughter handicapped? Does it have something to do with religion?"

"No one seems to know," she replied. "But he's so devoted. God knows we need more men like him."

I imagined Mr. Pierre, cheating in the rough, then tried to imagine him speaking to the City Council. A picture had indeed appeared in the *Des Moines Register*.

Then I went away to Europe, lost track of the story; at some point Susan, Nancy's older sister, became a hairdresser and my mother started going to her.

"Does Susan have *Playboy* magazines in her waiting room?" I asked one summer, fingering a few unruly stands of hair in my mother's permanent. "And does she do as good a job?"

My mother scowled.

In a moment I added:

"But what puzzles me is that you switched hairdressers. Did Mr. Pierre retire? Did you feel obligated to Susan?"

My mother, without saying a word, made it clear that for some unknown reason nothing more about Mr. Pierre would ever again be said in our house.

The Penis

I was seven or nine, perhaps even fourteen. I cannot remember whether I had pubic hair. My penis was infected: several painful boils, just below the glans.

In the hospital it was a young woman doctor who arrived in the tiny room where my father and I had been asked to wait. Wearing only my underpants, I was lying on the examination table. The woman doctor came around to the right side of the table and, delicately, pulled down the front of my underpants. She lifted my penis into the air.

She bent over it quite closely and studied the boils. She ran the tip of her index finger over one of them; then back again. It hurt when she did this, but at the same time her fingertip was cool, in a comforting, also ticklish way. I felt a rash spreading over my face. I was embarrassed and (as if I were standing alongside my father, observing myself on the examination table) curious about how a boy like me would react, when examined intimately by a woman doctor.

Other doctors—all young men—had by now come in. Gathered around her, they looked on, unsmiling, but with apparent interest. One of them asked a question; the woman doctor answered, turning to him while holding my penis between her thumb and index finger. She started gesturing towards my penis. I closed my eyes, anticipating something unpleasant that was about to happen (probably pain). And in a moment I felt on my lower abdomen the breath—I opened my eyes—of one of the young men, who had also wanted to get a closer look. A few of the others approached, but remained at a slightly greater distance.

I don't really know why—well, actually, I think I know why—from time to time I recall that morning spent at the hospital: my infected penis, the woman doctor, the warmth of the rash spreading across my cheeks, the soothing salve that the woman doctor applied and asked me to continue to apply for at least a week.

The Rented House

I woke up at four in the morning, couldn't sleep, went to the living room and read. Towards dawn I felt sleepy again, got up from the couch, looked out the window at the high-rise apartment buildings in the distance—the sky behind them was a dark luminescent blue—went back to the bedroom and fell asleep. I dreamt that we had rented a house in an entangled woods, and in the dream as well I awoke early. I got up, left the house, crossed the backyard, stepped across the stones of a stream. On the far side, standing amidst the branches of a large bush, I watched an animal slowly moving away, a raccoon I think. It stopped, turning its head; its eyes glistened in the moonlight. Later I saw a small pony, so small it was the size of a toy, galloping away. Now it was dawn; vapors were rising from the gently flowing water, from the dew on the weeds and high grass of the yard.

When I returned to the rented house I found three or four Gypsy children roaming about the back entrance. They wanted to go up an outer stairway, which led to the bedroom where Françoise was sleeping.

"Don't go up there," I explained to them. "We've rented the house for the summer."

On the other side of the house, women were setting out rugs and copper-wares to sell. They were obese women, covered with garish bracelets, necklaces, and wearing long faded dresses and black crocheted shawls. I noticed a road in front of the house; the house was in fact a roadside attraction.

"Françoise will not at all be happy when she learns that we have rented such a house for our vacation," I said to myself.

There was a similar stairway on that side of the house and up it I went. Two Gypsy children followed me.

"Menete kato!" I said to them in Greek. "Stay downstairs!"

It was a language which I had learned years before, then somewhat forgotten, but which I again spoke naturally, fluently.

The children giggled and ran back down, disappearing around a corner.

Hesitating at the top of the stairs, on a small wooden landing, I heard Françoise stirring.

"Are you getting up?" I asked through the pane of glass in the door.

Silence, but more stirring, the rustle of covers and sheets pushed away.

At this point I dreamt that the dream was over, but still perplexing was that period of time during which I had read, an hour or so which no seemed unreal. I remembered my book, remembered also the deep, dawn-expectant blue of the sky.

Into the room the sunlight was streaming, warming the wool covers of the bed.

I got up, went to the living room, confirmed that my book was still lying there, face down, near the couch upon which I read when I am worried and can't get to sleep.

The Food Stand

I felt a sudden urge to own commercial property. A food stand at a Parisian train station, for example, imagining myself serving up coffee to commuters in the early morning, their slow (or hasty) turning of the spoon in the cup. And almost as soon as I imagined this curious scene and felt on my cheeks and on the back of my hand the cold, drafty air of the Gare du Nord, I began wondering, worrying, about the wearing down of my things. The refrigerator that I would procure, the coffee machine, the aluminum top of the bar—would such things (my things) last forever?

And of course they would not. But my daydream (while I was sipping on a coffee at a stand at the Gare du Nord) had left me with the impression that things lasted forever. The impression was so strong that I accepted it as the truth, returning in my mind several times to the daydream, going over every detail that I could remember, discovering that picking up the plastic cup with the burning liquid inside helped me to do so. Feeling the warmth in my fingertips, squinting through the rising steam, I could almost imagine myself, once again, serving at my stand.

I was the owner of commercial property; my things would last forever.

And while sipping on the coffee (and making room for a new arrival at the bar)—while struggling to retain the fading daydream—I felt gathering like storm clouds all around me an immense sadness. These feelings were just outside my mind (and my body). I could perceive their billowing darkness; were it not for the immensity of the Gare du Nord, I think I would have felt trapped in a pressure cooker.

So I gave up. It was useless to continue. I gave in to the clouds, expecting death, and just as soon as I had accepted death the clouds vanished. There was no more pressure, but death was everywhere. Everywhere!

And, strangely, I felt almost serene.

I thought:

I was going to die someday, but I was not yet dead. I was not going to die in the immediate future; at least, not in the very next instant.

Why is it that I have to follow myself along such trains of thought, before the world can seem, simply—the steam rising from the cup of black coffee—miraculous?

Why Do I Imagine?

I found a mark in a book last night, which showed my father had read to page 83. John Berryman's *Love & Fame* (not *The Dream Songs*), which I had lent him. He had taken it in hand, looking over my books.

"Take it back to the hotel, Dad," I had said.

He was in town all alone, had breakfast with us. Croissants, pains aux raisins, from the bakery that opened at seven. In that apartment on the rue Albert-Bayet, in which we lived for nine years, the blackbirds woke us every morning at dawn.

Unable to sleep last night, I thought of my father, then of John Berryman, and took down the books from the shelf. I leafed through *The Dream Songs*, then *Love & Fame*, skimming over poems, reading a few carefully, thinking about suicide. Violent images engaged me, almost as if I were someone else. Lacerations, leaps off balconies, the ultimate instant of pain—my pain and someone else's; my life, my death, and someone else's.

Why, so fearful of pain in calmer moments, so afraid of the suffering that one day will come, do I imagine myself dying only thus—by my own hand, brutally?

Aux Marais d'Isle

When I couldn't live happily anymore, I started going to the Marais d'Isle in the late afternoon, to walk slowly over the soggy peat paths in search of something I could neither clearly define, nor designate. There were rarely others about that winter—a fisherman or two where the Somme widens, a lonely widow throwing bread to the moorhens and black coots, a retired couple strolling their dog in the allée bordering the marshland—and I was glad of the solitude that usually was mine once I had gone down the narrow path running alongside the railroad tracks and had entered the reserve itself. That narrow path with its chain-link fence on both sides and the occasional train rumbling over the rails on the embankment above formed an initiatory passage into what I intended to be—whoever arrived, whatever happened—my humanless hinterland, my refuge. Sometimes schoolchildren crowded noisily into the reserve and I would sit on a bench in a clearing off to the side until their teacher had herded them on. When amorous couples approached, I felt the pressure of our coexistence like a burning stare on my turned cheek, until at last we had passed in opposite directions.

It was the winter when I felt time slipping through my fingers. I found myself bringing my left hand up in front of me, palm open and facing upwards, and as I continued down the path I would recall for the hundredth time that disquieting young woman in the black-lace dress—my best friend's paramour—who at the going-away party he had given for me twenty years before had recited a poem, which ended:

> *And the poet with the broken lifeline*
> *is off to seek his fortune . . .*

As always, I would try to drive the verses from my mind. I often stopped along the sodden trail, reached out to touch the desiccated plants—sedge, bulrush, wild iris. The fragile, faded stems quivered, in a whispering breeze, against my fingertips. As a child, I would pick off leaves and break off twigs, then crumble the waxy, resinous substance between my thumb and forefinger. Now I examined the veins, the fibers, the fractured, withered surfaces, and left the leaves to an inexorable, but less brutal, disintegration. With the toe of my shoe I would nudge at the soil, the sludge from which these natural things had sprung, then gently trace a curving line. Then stop tracing. Then walk on.

Day came late, night fell early. I had never been so aware of the coming of the darkest days of winter. The rented apartment had become unbearable with its naked light bulbs burning all morning long, with its creaking wooden floors, with its kitchen linoleum scratched by the stiletto heels of the previous tenant, with its drafty, warped windows that shut only by forceful shoving. A traveling salesman lived in the apartment below, and when he returned well after midnight from his forays he would turn on the stereo, pace back and forth, open and shut doors, talk to himself. I slept restlessly anyway, but if he awakened me sleep was gone for hours and sometimes I switched on the night-light and read until nearly daybreak.

In the marshland, I sought to postpone the anticipation of night. By contemplating the sun sinking between the mossy branches of the alders, willows and birches, I could not force time to stand still; but by perceiving time passing I slowed its pace. My present was full of past things, future things—ceaselessly the same voices, faces, places, events arose. But like a rotting, life-generating, perpetually metamorphosing humus, my present was incorporating, as I strolled through the woods, precious instants of an incalculably vaster present otherwise remote from myself. I would breathe in the cool, moist vapors of the stagnant water, seeking to distinguish the mingled effluvia rushing through my nostrils; then hold my breath for as long as possible.

One afternoon, just as the sun was setting and I was walking out of the reserve, I noticed a solitary heron flying heavily, slowly, in a straight line, over the tops of the trees. It circled the Somme and its backwaters once, twice, passing above me each time, then glided massively down towards the distant shore. It alighted on the muddy bank, in a brief but mighty flapping of its majestic wings, then immediately adopted an upright posture. Its body was perched high and top-heavy on its spindly legs. After a long moment, however, the heron revealed itself to be supple, indeed nearly feline, and waded delicately, step by step, into the shallow water.

It came to a halt, a few feet out from the bank, and remained there, perfectly motionless. Only its head moved from time to time, the silhouette of its long beak visible to the left and then—as if I had daydreamed despite my conscious scrutiny while its head had turned—to the right. Sometimes, in the shadows cast by the passing clouds, the heron's ash-colored body disappeared while its long neck became a white stake rising from the murky river bottom.

The breeze had dwindled to a compelling stillness; the tiny siskins above me—migrators like myself—had ceased their chirping; only a dead leaf or two cracked underfoot as I shifted slightly. The hibernal sunlight traversed the bare woods far to my right, the pale yellow rays passing above the sheen of the dark river. Nothing else but the water stirred; on neither my side nor the heron's of the veil of haze was there a tremor. For what must have been a very long time, I waited for a fish—any fish—to swim by in its utter unknowingness, waited for the immobile heron to snap down at its prey with sureness and alacrity. I waited, wondering: Was my life going to change?

Vassilis

In Paris for the day, I ran into an old friend: a Greek writer. He was much older now, almost an old man. But he seemed in excellent health: fit and trim, tall—much taller than I remembered him, even taller than I.

"Vassilis," I said, "it's been such a long time. Comment vas-tu?"

He said he was all right, but I perceived in his eyes a sadness beyond telling. "On prend un pot?" he suggested.

I had a class, I had no time to have a drink with him. (Apparently, I was a student.)

We were in a Métro—or a RER—station. I needed to change trains. Yet we were also at an exhibition of abstract paintings. An exhibition organized by the RATP?

Vassilis and I walked slowly out of the gallery, back into a large open area. A panel overhead displayed departures. People were rushing every which way, sometimes jostling us.

We made sure we had each other's telephone number. Then we said good-bye, sadly, as if it were for the last time.

We glanced at each other, our eyes met for an instant, Vassilis stepped backwards, making a slight wave, a sort of salute. He turned, traversed with difficulty the hurried, crisscrossing movements of the crowd.

I had a class. Why? What kind of class? I looked at my ticket.

I was supposed to go to a small town in California: Rayon? Raon? This absurdity awakened me. I got out of bed. I searched in the darkness for a piece of scratch paper. I wrote this dream down.

I have just written this dream down and still feel that I need to turn and call out Vassilis's name, above the hustle and bustle of the commuters—"Vassilis!"—knowing that I something to say to him that will now never be said.

The Elevator

I was with a friend. I pushed the button, the elevator went down, continued past the second floor, the first floor, the ground floor, "I don't understand," I said, the elevator continued to go down, past the basement floors, "there are three basement levels," the elevator continued to go down.

It was a tiny elevator, two people only, my friend placed her hands against the sides. "What's wrong?" I asked. "What's happening?" She pushed harder, then I noticed the sides of the elevator collapsing inwards, flimsy sides, aluminum siding, detaching at the top.

The elevator continued to go down.

We continued to go down, both of us pushing as hard as we could against the collapsing sides, pushing as hard as we could, the elevator heading downwards, tears streaming from my friend's eyes. I screamed.

We continued to go down.

I screamed.

I awoke.

It was 6:04.

I calmed myself, calmed my beating heart.

Listened to a car swishing up the street.

Listened to the clock ticking in the other room.

Listened to Françoise breathing.

She was sleeping soundly, my scream had not awakened her. I rolled over, watched her sleeping, rolled back the other way. I listened to her breathing.

Through the crack in the curtains, light from the office building next door.

The cleaning ladies had arrived. I imagined them having their first coffee of the day together; their gestures, animated; talking all at once; one of them laughing, the others laughing in turn.

I remembered my nightmare.

I went over it in every detail: the elevator going down, my screaming. As if from afar this time, as if from outside myself, I felt myself talking again, felt the fright spreading, felt myself screaming.

As if from afar, as if from outside myself.

And felt from afar, felt from outside myself, I was just any human being—talking, feeling, perceiving—the tiniest, most fragile movements, no longer my own, movements that suddenly seemed so beautiful.

So beautiful.

With a peace I hadn't felt for weeks, months, perhaps years, I lay in bed until the alarm rang, then got up at once.

Mimi

We met in September on a blind date that began at seven p.m. and ended at ten-thirty. Months later, at the beginning of the second semester, Mimi turned up in my calculus class. She waited for me after the bell and, as if nothing had happened, indeed as if we were long-lost friends, asked about my classes, about my trip home for Christmas, about Charlie who had been in an automobile accident—the only thing we had talked about to any extent—whether he had recovered. We walked around the Administration Building, across the lawn, under the trees. I was ten minutes late for my next class because I accompanied Mimi all the way to her sorority.

In little time we were meeting once or twice a week to solve math problems. Mimi would "pop over," as she said, book and folder in hand, a red scarf draped around her neck. Her given name was Michele, but the diminutive was her smile, the sparkle in her brown eyes, her conviviality; also the shyness the conviviality concealed. Mimi would stamp the snow off her boots, "brrrr!" theatrically, step across the doorsill, take off her coat, toss it over the back of the armchair as if our apartment were hers. Charlie thought she was using me.

It is true we met more and more often. Mimi showed me her French compositions before handing them in; I helped her write an essay for a summer job (which she didn't get) at the statehouse in Boise. She never called in advance, she knocked on the door; even if she hadn't come by ten I would tell Charlie, Geoff and Mike to go without me for a pizza. Sometimes Mimi came, just to say hello, at eleven.

What I craved to know but didn't dare to ask was whether Mimi still went out from time to time with others; or whether she had a boyfriend back in Idaho Falls, a high-school flame rekindled at Christmas. Charlie insisted on her tainted reputation, that the previous fall she had slept "with the entire Phi Delt' House."

"I heard you were going out with Mimi," remarked Lou Meggs as I let him cut in line in the cafeteria of the Student Union.

"Not really going out with her," I replied. "We've become close friends."

The word "friendship" ate away at me.

One evening, rolling a pencil back and forth across the pages of her book, Mimi looked up and said:

"My life has changed. All that matters to me now is spending time with you, this way."

"This way" meant that our emotional intimacy grew, while in everyday life Mimi remained a mystery. What would it be like to see Mimi brushing her hair in the morning? To do the dishes with her? To help her pick out a pair of jeans? She talked in confidential detail about her brother, who the year before had married and was now getting a divorce. But when one night she asked me to make a cup of tea I felt uneasy in the kitchen downstairs because suddenly I was unsure whether my way of making tea was the same as hers. We never went out, not even for a snack at The Nest. Sometimes I asked: a production of *Uncle Vania*, a walk up near the golf course. Mimi had her excuses. She only let me walk her home, up a snow-packed Maple Street, to the Kappa House. Mimi would say:

"I've never felt so relaxed with a boy."

I would reply:

"I've never felt so relaxed with a girl."

To keep from slipping, Mimi would grip the sleeve of my coat.

One night, however, she suddenly put her head on my shoulder. No one was home; a Friday night; Mimi and I were sitting on the bed, looking up words in the French dictionary. She laughed a little, covered her mouth; I put the dictionary aside and kissed her forehead. We sat like that for a while, my arm around her; then we lay back on the bed.

We held on to each other, kissing from time to time, Mimi warm and giggly. I touched her cheek, we kissed again; when I moved my hand to her breast she moved my hand away. The pale light from the distant street; along the wall a veil of light; light nearer shadow than light; the sound of Mimi's breathing; then her sudden laugh as she blew in my ear; I touched her breast again and this time she unbuttoned her blouse; I slipped my hand underneath; I slowly glided my fingers across the silken fabric of her bra. We held on to each other; we kissed, in a while our caresses stopped and we only kissed, our hands clasped between us. Came the first warm moments of sleep. Mimi kissed my nose, shook me, asked to be taken home. It was three o'clock in the morning.

"Stay, Mimi," I said.

Mimi gave my nose another kiss, then climbed over me and out of bed.

A few minutes later, on the porch of the Kappa House, I whispered in Mimi's ear:

"I love you."

She woke us at nine o'clock the next morning. From her look I knew what was coming; I slipped on my coat; we walked in silence down the flight of stairs, between the parked cars, down Railroad Street, towards the Student Union. I put my arm around Mimi and asked her what the matter was.

She said: "I want things to return to normal."

I did my best to acquiesce; that is, I pretended I had acquiesced.

March, April, May—we were inseparable. Finals came. Mimi, except for sleeping, lived with us. She brought over her toaster; in the evenings, to stay awake, we made instant coffee, cooked tapioca. We covered my tiny blackboard with calculus proofs. We memorized them, we recited them. The night before the exam, at two in the morning, we walked to the other end of campus, near the new dormitories.

"I've decided to stay for summer school," I announced. "Maybe I'll be able to find a ride down to Idaho Falls to see you some weekend."

Mimi nodded, smiled, bit her lower lip.

When we returned to the apartment she collapsed on the bed. I continued studying, if only to watch over her. I covered her with the bedspread; I watched her turning over; at eight I rubbed her back until she awoke.

Two days later I was putting her suitcases in the trunk of a girlfriend's car. When I had finished, Mimi hugged me, turned me to and fro. In a moment she stepped back, touched my nose. She opened the door, got in. She rolled down the window, placed her arm on the sill. I squeezed her arm, then our fingers met, gripped together.

"Write," said Mimi.

"You too."

Our hands shook that way, just the fingers gripping.

"I'll call you, too," I added as the motor started.

We let go of each other.

The car disappeared so quickly!

Just as quickly I'll end this love story: the other fellow in Idaho Falls.

∞

Five years later, after I had moved (temporarily) to Greece, I noticed in the same alumni magazine which I have received for years, which always catches up with me wherever I go, although I have never taken out a subscription or sent in a change of address, that Mimi had given birth to a child. Strangely, the news provoked violent feelings. I felt betrayed, jealous, even somehow impotent. It was early in the morning. A donkey was braying. I was sitting at my desk, in the cold house I was renting in the village.

When I finally realized how ridiculous I was, I calmed down. Later that day I decided to write Mimi a letter. I congratulated her on the birth, asked about her life in Portland (the city mentioned in the announcement), went on for pages about that special year.

"I always wondered what happened to you," I wrote, "after you started going to Idaho State."

I tried to keep the tone slightly distant, but could not long resist evoking my old affections. More or less everything I have recalled here wound up in the letter, including the part about our one night of tenderness.

"I'll never forget that night as long as I live," I remember writing, imagining how Mimi might react when she read my description.

I no longer had her address, but still had Steve's; he would know where to find her. I selected an airmail envelope, folded the letter, put the letter in the envelope. I wrote out Mimi's *maiden* name, then Steve's name and address underneath. I licked an airmail stamp (depicting the Parthenon), stuck it on the envelope very carefully, making sure that the edges of the stamp were perfectly parallel to those of the envelope. I sighed. I had the impression that I was about to perform some solemn, definitive act.

I left my cold house, walked down the steep cobblestone path to the small square, hesitated for a moment, looked around—several old villagers, sitting inside the café, were watching me—then slid the letter through the narrow opening into the iron mailbox—from which a postman collected the mail once a week, at best—sure (almost sure) that I would never receive a reply from Mimi, nor ever see her again.

Joe

I have just watched a man carrying a pail of cement across the rue de Belgique and started thinking about Joe Jaharis. He was my first roommate in college, but only for three or four weeks. After Charlie, Mike and Geoff and I proved he had been stealing change from my wallet, which I kept in the right top-hand drawer of my desk whenever I was sleeping or going to the shower down the hall, Joe moved in with someone else—or was it into a single room? In any case he stopped tagging along with us—to Rathskeller's, the student beer hall located a mile or so out of town.

A year went by, Joe and I drifted apart, but never so far apart that he wouldn't knock on my door, stand in the doorway and recount his latest in-fatuations. Joe's love stories never told of exploits, sieges, conquest, but instead of the precise corporal attributes of such and such a girl whom he had seen on campus or, of course, at Rathskeller's, to which he would walk alone nearly every night, along the dusty shoulder of the state highway, edging over to the deep ravine whenever headlight beams came rushing up from behind. As for us, having squeezed into Geoff's shiny Volkswagen, sometimes we drove past him on that road, not one of us offering even a wave and later, at Rathskeller's, making it clear to him that he was not welcome at our table. (How I remember Geoff's well-tuned Volkswagen, with its thin, lightweight, but extraordinarily sturdy doors that he admonished us never to slam! If all the windows were up, you would feel a sudden, unpleasant pop in your ear—because of the hermetically sealed interior.)

Joe, who had no car and few possessions, was simply too ugly to attract girls. His high and wide cheekbones made his face seem oval, horizontally so; his jaw receded with respect to his thick upper lip; above and around his lip spread a narrow, sparse moustache; his eyebrows were incredibly bushy. He had a flabby, languorous, vulnerable look about his whole body; when he was younger, many a half-teasing, half-nasty punch must have landed in his soft belly.

Joe would ask girls to dance at Rathskeller's, getting up cautiously but not uncourageously from the table at which he had already drunk three or four

beers all by himself, lumbering over to a table full of giggling, already inebri-
ated girls from Washington State University, located across the nearby state
line (where the drinking age was still twenty-one), standing behind the most
beautiful one—although I often counseled him to be less picky—until she
had acknowledged his presence, a turning-of-head-and-shoulder which took
some time since Joe was not someone you noticed immediately, except as an
object of derision. Then, in mumbled words, almost a monologue, Joe would
ask her to dance. What exactly did he feel, I wondered then and still wonder
today, when the entire table of girls burst into laughter?

All Joe's love stories were replete with this profound sadness. I remember
one in particular, involving a trip to Spokane.

It began at Rathskeller's, when at last Joe had convinced a girl to dance with
him. She had "a fuckin' pair of boobs," as he put it; they danced once; in order
to get rid of him (as I quickly understood while he was telling me the story;
he did not draw this conclusion), she said that she couldn't dance with him
anymore but that if he wanted to, he could visit her in Spokane. The girl, who
was still in high school, was visiting her sister in Moscow; Spokane was a two-
hour drive away; no one would have lent Joe a car; how could the girl imagine
that Joe would take the bus?

And how would she imagine that Joe, who knew only her first name (Sue)
and had miraculously overheard the name of the high school, would find her
in a city of 200,000 people?

He spent the morning and early afternoon wandering the streets around
the high school, asking all sorts of people if they knew a Sue, knocking on
door after door as potential Sues were suggested, never giving up, finally
being pointed up a long winding street in obviously the newest and richest
section of the suburb, a street—let's call it "Belmont Heights Drive"—lined
with neo-colonial homes set back on sloping lawns spotted with fir and maple
seedlings. A man driving his tractor-mower in front of one of the houses was
Sue's father.

Thinking back on Joe telling me this—he was standing in the doorway of the
room that I then shared with Mike; I was sitting at my desk, only half turned
around to him—I remember that up to this point I hardly believed a word of
his story. What followed was even less believable, yet must have been true.

The man agreed that his Sue answered the description. But then he said that
she had gone out. He walked back to his mower, got on, started it, drove off to
cut more grass. Joe sat down on the curb. After a while, the man returned to

the middle of the lawn and set up a sprinkler. Water soon sprouted out of the whirling sprinkler in vast arcs.

"I got pretty wet," explained Joe.

Joe had gotten up, walked across the street, sat down on the other curb. Presumably he had dried off by the time Sue, driving her parents' car, turned into the double driveway.

The next scene took place in the living room, into which ("a really embarrassed," Joe admitted) Sue invited him. Looks were exchanged between mother and father and daughter; Joe was served a glass of water, perhaps a Coke; Sue asked:

"... a lot of stupid questions about how things were going in Moscow, about my classes, about the bus trip, about the people in the bus. I kept trying to work the subject around to our relationship. I reached for her hand once but she got up and went into the kitchen. I thought it was for something to eat—I was starving—but instead she came back after quite a while empty-handed and sat down in the armchair across from the couch. I gestured at her to come over next to me..."

Joe showed me how he had beckoned her over; his extended fingers curled inward and made a squeezing movement; he laughed lewdly.

"... then I heard a car roaring up the street, I mean a real dragster. The car turned into Sue's driveway. It was her boyfriend..."

I asked Joe what the boyfriend was like.

He was muscular, wore a sleeveless T-shirt. A blue-jean jacket, held by a finger, was draped over his right shoulder.

With undisguised admiration, Joe gave me the complete description, imitating (by crossing the threshold of my own room) the boyfriend ambling cockily into the living room, glaring at him.

"Who are you?" he had barked at Joe before Sue could introduce them.

"... we sat there for a moment, the three of us, I had moved into the armchair, Sue and her boyfriend were sitting closely on the couch, looking at each other all the time, not a word was spoken. Then they left..."

"Left?"

"They had a date."

"What happened then?"

She's father had disappeared, but Sue's mother came into the living room, sat down, chatted with Joe for quite some time. She made a couple of sandwiches for him, for the road. He hitchhiked back to Moscow.

After that, I rarely saw Joe. By the next year Charlie, Mike, Geoff and I moved off campus. Besides, we had stopped going to Rathskeller's and now hung out at Mort's, a much smaller student bar located near Main Street.

This is why I was surprised, the day after Thanksgiving during my senior year, when Joe telephoned me at my grandmother's, in Lewiston. I had gone down to visit her for a few days—how in the world did Joe find me there?

He was hitchhiking his way back up from southern Idaho and was looking for a place to spend the night. Remembering that someone in my mother's family had a real-estate office in Lewiston, Joe tried them all until he hit the right one. One of my uncles, closing up, let him use the office telephone.

Joe arrived; my grandmother and I showed him to the guest room; we ate dinner; my grandmother (always delighted to have guests) announced she would make her famous orange rolls for breakfast.

"Don't worry about me," she said. "Why don't you go out for a bit?"

Joe and I went downtown for a beer.

We entered a place called Jekyll & Hyde's, a new type of chain pizza parlor and student bar; another had recently opened in Moscow. More sedate than the raucous Rathskeller's or Mort's, Jekyll & Hyde's had only a small dancing area in the middle; most of the booths and tables were only for two people; not only the floor, but also the walls and the ceiling were carpeted; candles burned inside red or green-tinted glass holders; everything was rather dark except when the person in charge of the disco music turned on the strobe lights.

I don't remember what Joe and I talked about. Something tells me it was not about girls; maybe it was about his grades; he was flunking out of business school, as I learned somewhat later from Lou Meggs. Perhaps I told Joe I could help him with the calculus requirement; perhaps I told him I didn't have much time.

Which I didn't. Such a busy year that last one in college was.

I remember feeling that my entire evening was being wasted. Joe wanted to order another beer; after two or three, I told him that we had better go back up the steep hill to my grandmother's house.

Which we did.

But now, fifteen years later and in a foreign country, after watching a worker carrying a pail of cement across the rue de Belgique—they're finally renovating the low-cost housing units next-door—I have started thinking about Joe, wondering what has become of him. How strange it is. I think I would really like to know.

Thirst

It must have been five o'clock in the morning, this morning. I awoke with a strange pasty sensation in my mouth. I ran the tip of my tongue over my palate. The skin there was swollen; the crests and crater rims of the palate, swollen. In what seemed to be a mere moment I realized that several moments must have gone by, even that I had fallen back asleep, slept for an hour, awakened again: the skin covering the palate was no longer swollen. I toyed with the idea of getting up. In the meantime I had become less afraid of whatever it was that had awakened me. Yes, I had been afraid—that now I knew. It had not been a dream; it had been something belonging to the real world immediately outside. I listened to the sounds of the night . . . until a car turned, rushed down our street, screeched to a halt—eight stories down below. A door slammed. A young woman shouted: "Ciao!" I was suddenly very thirsty.

The Bon Ton

None of us children standing outside what was then George's Super Valu ever managed to see anyone entering the sinister little tavern across Urbandale Avenue, or leaving it, but through the tinted window we would make out a burning light bulb and on the side of the dingy building an air-conditioner ran continuously. Rumors had reached us and kept us waiting there, that one night at The Bon Ton there had been a fight with broken-off beer bottles, that the police had raided and found a roulette wheel, even that there had been a shooting. Only once, in Beaverdale on an errand for my mother, did I find the door of The Bon Ton open. A man brought out the garbage. Later he pushed a vacuum cleaner around the entrance, finally locked up, looked around, went away. I had seen a bar and barstools in the background, a booth or two up front. And that was all.

I asked my father about The Bon Ton.

But he had never given it much thought, didn't really know who went there. "Maybe Mr. Manson?" I suggested.

"No, no, not him!" he replied so quickly that thereafter it was precisely Mr. Manson whom I imagined sitting in a corner booth, sweat showing on his T-shirt, a pack of Camels rolled up into this sleeve. His hands were clasped under his chin; his face was expressionless; he was staring into the darkness.

And in that darkness were other faces, but to which I could give no names.

The Bon Ton was located around the corner from the shops and stores to which my friends and I, my parents and I, went often: Elsie's, Clayton's, Jerry's Shoes, Reed's Ice Cream. In later years, walking with friends up Beaver Avenue after school, I would steal a glance at the tavern, seemingly closed up except for the pale sheen of the light bulb in the dark window, though by that age I felt that I shouldn't be looking at the tavern, for to be caught looking at it when the others were not, and even if the others did not say anything, was to be caught imagining the things that went on inside, indeed caught doing the things that went on inside—yet I couldn't keep myself from looking. Often I imagined myself entering the tavern and somehow standing invisibly at the very center of whatever sordid world it contained, my hands nervously withdrawn from my pockets and my eyes slowly moving from face to face. I was eleven years old.

Ten years later (when for the first time I could have entered a tavern legally), The Bon Ton became the nightly hangout for a few of my old friends. With some of them I had ridden the bench on our high-school basketball team; several of them I had known since grade school. By now they had dropped out of college: a few were selling cars or refrigerators; two or three were dealing drugs.

Or so I had heard.

I had gone away to college and came back home only once or twice a year, for vacations.

It was Craig whom most of all I would have liked to see again. Many events, many words, had linked our lives together for years. But fear and incertitude kept me away; at Margie's wedding the previous summer, she had whispered to me at the reception:

"I went to see him, to tell him. It's terrible what's happened to him, but I can't do anything."

Someone swept Margie back to the festivities.

As to Craig, I can still see him entering the living room, where Margie, Donni and I were talking with Margie's parents. It was six o'clock; soon we would be leaving for the senior prom. Craig looked at Margie, then at Donni, suddenly realizing he had forgotten to buy a corsage. Margie took it pretty well; Craig and I left the girls, hopped in his car, sped to Boesen's. The flower shop was just closing. Mr. Boesen let us in. He was gentle, understanding, even a little sad. Orchid corsages need to be ordered at least two weeks in advance.

"Let me see what I can do," he said.

He whipped up a corsage out of odds and ends. It was actually quite beautiful. There was a lot of curly ribbon, a bit of fern and at least one miniature rose. He gave it to Craig without asking him to pay; back at Margie's house, she pinned it on, saying it was lovely. But I saw what she thought. I also saw what her parents thought. And what had been said about Craig while we were gone? I do not recall whether one of Margie's girlfriends, at the dance, made a nasty remark in the powder room of the Savery Hotel. Something tells me that happened too.

The forgotten corsage marked the beginning of the end of Craig and Margie's relationship. No couple at Hoover High School had been together longer—since seventh grade. When Craig announced the news to me in the cafeteria, trying to slough it all off, he mentioned that he and Margie had been secretly engaged for over a year. Engaged! There had been a ring! Margie had kept it hidden from everyone, even from Donni. Margie's parents detested Craig; who knows what would have happened if they had known?

"I've got to find a way of selling the ring," he said. "I had Margie's name engraved on the inside. The jeweler's where I bought it won't buy it back. All my summer savings went into it and my parents think I've still got that money saved up for college."

I looked at Craig, unable to make the slightest suggestion. At that precise instant we became adults.

Whatever happened to that ring?

The question is futile, I know, but I am sad today, remembering all this.

In the elevator this morning, on my way back up from the letterbox—empty, the mailman was late again—I suddenly remembered that silver ring with its tiny diamond. I don't know why I remembered it: my hands were empty; I had spoken to no one; I had pushed the button; the elevator was gliding upwards, with its usual humming sound. Usually I think of nothing; time passes; and I am aware of its passing. But into my mind came Craig; he sat down beside me, took the ring from the front pocket of his jeans and, underneath the cafeteria table, held it out for an instant. The tiny diamond sparkled. He turned the ring. He showed me Margie's name.

Then he put the ring away, we finished eating, we put our trays in the racks, we went off to English class.

For reasons I could not that noon have imagined, I broke up with Donni at the end of the week. We graduated, we went our separate ways—Craig, Margie, Donni and I.

Craig? Donni? I never saw them again. Margie I saw at her wedding; then again ten years ago, briefly, when my mother died.

It was a day or two after the funeral. Margie had dropped by with her husband; they were sitting across from me, on the living-room couch. We were joking about old times . . . when, painfully, strangely, perhaps because of my mother's death—I am not really sure—there was nothing else to say.

Eyebrows

I remember that curious caress, the tip of her nose ruffling through my eyebrows, back and forth, back and forth. A funny, nervous, gentle loving, sometimes with laughs, exuberance; and the funny name we gave it: vacuuming.

Still-crisp February afternoons—at the Temple of Hera. "Behind the stone wall," we had whispered; where the terrain sloped downwards so that I was the shortest.

I had forgotten that feeling—heels perched above emptiness, the emptiness in my stomach and nerves, the trembling acceptance of her closeness, our desire. Just a week, but for minutes every afternoon, it lasted.

Now, fourteen years later, this mirror that brings me back to myself in those moments. When my cheeks warmed in the chilly, silent air. When my eyes were afraid, yet willing, and waiting. When I closed my eyes. Delicate sensations of long ago, the tickling and prickling of insignificant hairs.

Belle-Maman

For years she had intrigued me, that effervescent young mother, her four children in tow—"Be careful, children!" "Over this way, children! "Sé-bas-tien, will you please keep quiet!" "Claire, spit that out, right this minute!"—but it was only one morning when I noticed that rivulets of varnish had run down the white pipes in our bedroom, the ones in the far corner, between the two corner windows, that we spoke for the first time.

"Monsieur, I am very sorry," she said. "Actually, it was my husband who varnished his mother's wooden floor and he must not have noticed the hole. It was already so late last night and, despite what people say, doctors also have a right to a bit of relaxation. What I mean is that my husband is a surgeon. At the hospital he performs delicate operations all day long and then in the evening he has to pick up a paintbrush for his mother. My husband is of course happy to help her out, but there are limits to what one man can do. As for us, we live on the sixteenth floor. We also have a hole near the pipe—in the kitchen. When they built these high-rises—nothing but shoddy materials and sloppy workmanship! Not to mention the cockroaches. In Belle-Maman's apartment . . ."

I retained the expression and thereafter we nicknamed her precisely that: Belle-Maman, "Mommy-in-Law."

The next week we met her mother-in-law, the real Belle-Maman.

"Please tell me," she asked timidly after I had ushered her into the living room. "Do I disturb you?"

She was a small woman of about seventy, her white hair gathered into a chignon.

"I mean, do you hear noises coming from my apartment? I watch television, but I also read a lot. I knit. Maybe my washing machine bothers you?"

"No, not at all," replied Françoise.

"Well, can you imagine that the couple who lives above me told the house manager that I was a troublemaker?"

The real Belle-Maman explained how on several occasion she had been forced to complain about the noise her neighbors made: their flute-playing, their typewriting all night long (the sound waves conducted by the same bedroom pipes which, at our level, were now striped with varnish); above all, their inexcusable impoliteness, such as the time when she had asked them to turn down the stereo and the young man, a student of Slavic languages, had refused to speak French on the phone and shouted:

"Niet, niet, niet, niet, niet!"

"That young man I have never meet. Apparently, he has not been here a very long time. But Mademoisselle Brun—you may already know this—is an *agrégée*. I find it shameful that a teacher, who is supposed to provide children with a good example, acts so rudely to the elderly. I, myself, was a teacher."

Later that afternoon we knocked on Jean-Yves and Anne-Marie's door.

"You will never believe it," laughed Jean-Yves. "We come back from a movie, Anne-Marie starts filling up the tub for a bath—the old bitch calls. I decide to mix up a hot chocolate at midnight and accidently drop a spoon on the floor—the old bitch calls. They accuse us of making noises with our chairs, but, take a look, we don't have any chairs!"

Their living-room furniture consisted of several large cushions strewn in a corner.

"The daughter-in-law is completely hysterical," added Anne-Marie. "I'm sick and tired of women who have children!"

"We call her 'Belle-Maman,'" interjected Françoise. "But let's not go into that."

Not once had Jean-Yves and Anne-Marie met the real Belle-Maman. The dispute had gone on for months: by telephone, by registered mail; Huberto, the house manager (whom everyone called "Hubert"), had gotten involved; his wife Berthe as well.

"But she lives just one floor below you," pleaded Françoise. "It's senseless not to try to talk things out."

"All right, all right. We'll go down and see her," replied Jean-Yves.

Then he turned to me and, showing off still one more of his languages, said in almost perfect English:

"I know how to handle these old ladies."

That Christmas the real Belle-Maman left a card in our mailbox:

My son, my daughter-in-law, and my four grandchildren join me in wishing you a happy new year and in thanking you from the bottom of our hearts for intervening so kindly in the affair of which you are aware.

"You won't believe it," I announced to Françoise upon returning to the apartment. "A new year's card from Belle-Maman; that is, from the real Belle-Maman, from Belle-Maman, and from Fils!"

"Fils?"

But which one of the elevator personages was the real Belle-Maman's son; that is, Belle-Maman's husband?

We had come up with various candidates: the tall, middle-aged, English-looking fellow whom we later saw on the pont Neuf holding hands with a girl barely out of high school; or the man we called "Flic," but who suddenly packed up his bags and quite a stack of unpaid rent notices. Once I had even conjectured that Belle-Maman might be a single mother.

"Belle-Maman all alone, with four children?" Françoise had retorted.

Then, in a moment:

"Do you think it's possible?"

Not once had we seen Belle-Maman with a man, that is with Fils, Belle-Maman who every day walked her children (and most of the other children in the building) down the street to school, who then returned all in a bustle to the building, who then reappeared, shopping trolley in hand, the new baby still strapped to her chest in a Snugli carrier, dashing off this time to the supermarket, returning an hour later with food enough for a day or two, Belle-Maman who then made the beds and put the toys away, sponged off the kitchen table, vacuumed all the rooms, got the Ajax out and scrubbed the toilet, the bathtub, the bidet, having fed the baby in the meantime, Belle-Maman who then attacked the washing—some of the clothes by hand, of course—who ironed the clothes, folded them, Belle-Maman on whom the other mothers could count to get up promptly from her short afternoon nap and be at the entrance of the school at precisely 4:30 p.m. . . .

"I'm always there well ahead of time," I overheard her saying to Berthe one evening as I was returning from the newspaper kiosk. "Nowhere's safe these days, believe me."

"Do you really think so?"

"Oh yes! To the extent that we may soon be forced to put our children into private schools."

∞

One morning a man wearing a gray suit, a pinstripe shirt and a discreet tie spoke to me in the elevator. He was about forty years old. Though neither tall nor obese, his voice was deep and melodious.

"I would like to communicate my gratitude to you for the kindness you have displayed towards my mother, my wife, and my children."

"(Fils!) Don't mention it. It was nothing, nothing at all. How is the problem with your mother's neighbors coming along?"

"We are working our way towards a solution, Monsieur, thank you. As you know, my wife and my mother have been very upset about this matter."

What else was there to say? The elevator door opened, Fils graciously gestured me out, shook my hand, bade me good-bye, then hurried off to his operations.

After that, I ran into Fils often.

One Saturday night I at last saw them together. As the elevator doors opened, there was Fils and there was Belle-Maman, both magnificent in their evening attire, Fils in his new suit and shined shoes, Belle-Maman in her black dress and high-heels, her eyes thickly lined, her lips red, waxy, her cheeks rouged and powdery.

"Bonsoir, Monsieur!" she exclaimed as they left the elevator.

It was not just any Saturday night. Off they were going to the annual staff party at the Hôpital de la Pitié-Salpêtrière.

Slowly but surely our lives, if only slightly, had become entangled.

It was at this stage of our acquaintance that I came across Belle-Maman behind the building.

Returning from the supermarket, pulling her shopping trolley, she was crossing the small playground that tenants used as a shortcut to and from the avenue de Choisy.

"Bonjour," I said. "Ça va?"

Belle-Maman's look made me stop.

"No," she said, shaking her head. "Not at all."

My years in France had taught me not to inquire further; there was a short silence; then Belle-Maman said:

"I've got all sorts of problems."

"I'm sorry to hear that," I replied.

"It's nice of you to say that."

Belle-Maman continued on her way. I watched her pull open the cumbersome metal gate, maneuver with some difficulty her shopping trolley down the walk that led to the side entrance, then disappear.

"It's unbelievable," remarked Françoise when I told her what had happened, "that she confided in you in that way."

"Yes, yes, I agree. I can't explain it."

In May we learned we would have to move to Angers.

"We too are going to move!" Belle-Maman had exclaimed to Françoise while they were waiting for the elevator. "The money we have been saving up in our long-term account will soon be available. But how exhausting moving is! The boxes of books!"

"They have books?" I asked, later.

"And that's not all," continued Françoise. "Belle-Maman said . . ." (and Françoise imitated Belle-Maman's enthusiastic voice) ". . . Belle-Maman said: 'Can you believe it? All this work to finish before the month of August. Because my husband and I have always said that a vacation every year for the children is sacred! Let's hope that the house we are having built in the suburbs will be finished in time.'"

"Do you think that the real Belle-Maman will go and live with them?"

"I'm absolutely certain she will," replied Françoise.

"And what about Jean-Yves and Anne-Marie? How did that story finish up?"

A few months later, back in Paris for a short visit to see our friends, we learned that Belle-Maman was finding suburban life boring.

"What did you expect?" laughed Eve, who still lived in the building and often chatted with Berthe (who knew everything about the former and the present tenants). "She doesn't have the other women here to talk with anymore."

"She's going to suffer when all her children are at school during the day," added Dimitri, Eve's husband, "not to mention when they leave home for good."

Which made me think of my mother. I kept my sadness to myself, said nothing—what was there to say? My friends continued talking.

Françoise explained to Eve and Dimitri how nice Belle-Maman had been to her the day we left Paris, after one of the movers had been so vulgar and insulting.

∞

Since then, months have gone by. I have taken a long trip, returned; Françoise
has also had to travel. Friends have visited; now it's almost Christmas; we
hope to find at last some peace and quiet.

Yet Dimitri's words continue to haunt me.

In fact, I can't drive them away at all.

And sometimes I start daydreaming of Belle-Maman, as if by chance we
would run into each other on a street in Saint-Germain-des-Prés, on one of
those Tuesdays or Thursdays, every month or so, when I make a quick trip to
Paris.

"(. . .)"

"(. . .)"

"(. . .)"

"(. . .)"

"(. . .)"

"(. . .)"

"(. . .)"

"You're kidding! No, really, you should buy a car. The surrounding countryside is wonderful!"

"(. . .)"

"(. . .)"

"(. . .)"

"(. . .)"

"(. . .)"

"At the beginning, once or twice, but not anymore."

"(. . .)"

"(. . .)"

"(. . .)"

"Ah, you can't believe what it's like to go shopping for children!" she would
exclaim, showing me an incredible number of bags.

And that would be all.

Belle-Maman would go her way, I mine. But I know that such an encounter
would give me a feeling, however ephemeral, of security.

Childhood Sweetheart

Back in Des Moines after years in France, browsing for something to read in a hotel, I picked up a local magazine, opened it to the first page, came across her name on the masthead. Rachel was one of the contributing editors. When I turned to the article—about restoring homes on Sherman Hill, once part of the Black ghetto—I immediately recognized her brilliant style, her intimacy with the rarest words, her humor tinged with skepticism. I imagined her in Creston—a short note followed her name—thinking the move implied a divorce. (At last word she had married and moved to Pennsylvania.) Was she the editor of the Creston newspaper? I left the hotel, hurried down Locust Street to the Public Library.

In the Reference Room I found the back issues of the magazine. Rachel had been contributing articles for the past two years. I read what she had written about a new college in Storm Lake, about vacation homes; in the card catalog I discovered that she had coauthored a book—published in Pennsylvania—about alternatives to surgery. That would have been for money, I thought, remembering how Rachel detested science; though she, who had gone to bullfights in Spain, would not have been squeamish about the details.

There was no sign of a novel or a collection of stories.

For years I had wondered whether Rachel had continued writing, she who when so young had won so many prizes. Joan had asked me once, at a pizzeria in Paris.

"I've never seen anything of hers," I replied. "But then, I don't see many American books and magazines here. Could you find out for me?"

Joan forgot, and from time to time I remembered that she had forgotten.

Indeed I sometimes daydreamt, once I had begun reviewing books, that one of Rachel's had come my way, or vice versa; or that Rachel and I had been invited to a symposium, back in Des Moines, where we were wined and dined and then asked to debate. In such fantasies I feared her, feared her intelligence and feared her revenge, for when after joining me in Germany nothing had come of her hopes and she had returned to Des Moines, she had gone to see

my parents—many months later—and given them her side of the story. It was
that version which remained in the family; three years later my mother said:

"I was shocked by the way you brutalized her."

Rachel had explained to my parents that she was engaged to a journalist
and would soon move to Pennsylvania. She had added:

"At last I have learned I can love someone else."

I often thought about that remark in the years that followed, and always
with a certain bewilderment, as if unable to fathom its nonetheless obvious
meaning.

As to "brutalized," it was not really the word for what had happened in
Hamburg. Rachel had suddenly written to me—after seven months of silence—announcing her imminent arrival in Europe. Could she visit me, she
wanted to know? What could I answer but yes? I could no longer look forward
to seeing her; my love for her had once again faded, definitively as it turned
out; so much in my life had changed ever since I had left the States behind for
good. But hadn't Rachel and I been intimately linked for years? Not to mention that seven months before, we had been engaged: for one tumultuous day.

Yes, that day had been tumultuous and all too typical of the way Rachel's
life and mine would suddenly converge after months, after years, of separa-
tion—of resentment and bitterness, of occasional regret and longing. At the
time I was waiting to leave for Germany; I had won a scholarship; in a few
months I would be free to pursue a secret ambition, long postponed. So why,
one Friday morning at work, did I suddenly telephone Rachel, whom I had
not seen for over two years?

She was no longer living in Des Moines, as I learned from her mother, who,
I sensed, was not very happy to hear my voice again; she had come to distrust
these unexpected reappearances in her daughter's life.

"She's working for the Mason City newspaper," she explained.

I didn't ask for Rachel's home number and her mother offered no further
information. She said good-bye, politely, hung up. I found the number in the
phone book, called Rachel; she agreed to meet. There was only a little irony in
her voice this time; she actually seemed glad I had called. I drove up to Mason
City early the next morning.

Rachel did tell me, almost as soon as I had entered her apartment, that for
the past six months she had been going out with a reporter at the newspaper—
the one with whom she later went off to Pennsylvania?

By that afternoon, however, we had fallen in love all over again, kissing each other in a corner of a deserted public library and later back in her apartment. We agreed that I would drive up the following Saturday. I returned home that evening, euphoric; late the next afternoon the telephone rang: Rachel had driven down to Des Moines.

"I'm going to break up with Kenneth," she announced. "I've taken tomorrow off. I need to see you."

I asked my mother for the keys to the car, left the house in a trance, picked up Rachel at her parents' house. We decided to have dinner at a crêperie that had just opened on Forest Avenue.

When we sat down, Rachel admitted she wasn't hungry.

"I'm simply too nervous about us," she said.

I suggested we leave; Rachel insisted I order something; the waiter was indeed waiting, at our side. I ordered a vegetarian crêpe. Then, halfway through the spinach and broccoli and alfalfa sprouts, I suddenly looked up and asked Rachel to marry me. Just like that. It was the strangest, most spontaneous act I had ever performed in my life. I felt as if someone else had pronounced the words: I heard, saw, myself pronouncing them. And that someone else who had just proposed to his childhood sweetheart seemed happy—as if happy at last, after many past disappointments. Rachel immediately accepted, taking my hand in hers, drawing my finger to her lips. She started crying.

The first person we told was Rachel's grandmother, who that same year had moved up from Missouri and into a retirement home on Grand Avenue. She had always had a weak spot in her heart for me, defending my integrity (I suspected) against her son-in-law and especially her daughter, and perhaps even reassuring Rachel, whenever I suddenly showed up after months of absence, knocking on their front-porch door. We then drove back to Rachel's parents' house: her father congratulated us, but said nothing more; her mother asked whether we were really sure.

Rachel answered yes, aggressively.

At our house, my father was out of town until Tuesday; as to my mother, she said:

"I always knew this would happen."

But she, like Rachel's mother, seemed skeptical.

The next day Rachel and I decided to return to Mason City. I had already called in to work, requesting two days of vacation.

It was a two-hour drive on Interstate 35 and, by the time we had arrived at the Ames turnoff, twenty minutes north of Des Moines, I started feeling—

Rachel, too, as I was beginning to perceive—that our joy was not fully genu-ine. First, she was pulled over for speeding: 80 in a 55 mph zone. She argued with the patrolman; it took me quite a while to calm her down afterwards. Hoping to soothe her, I twice called her "Honey," whereas I had never called her anything but "Rachel" in the past.

After the second time, Rachel glanced at me painfully, then asked me never to use the term again.

"I always loved the way you called me 'Rachel,' even in junior high, even when my friends would call me 'Rache.'"

We said little after that. Rachel eventually stopped at a rest area. I got in behind the wheel.

In a moment, however, she began talking about Kenneth. She did not know how she would announce the news to him. They had been planning to live to-gether, had she told me that? What were we going to do about Germany? Did I really want to go? Her job at the newspaper? Her career? The miles went by: cornfields, soybean fields. Eventually Rachel confessed that she might still be in love with Kenneth, after all. Did I think it was possible to love two people at the same time?

We arrived in Mason City, thoroughly discouraged. There was no argument this time, just a profound weariness. Nine years spent trying to love each oth-er—and once again, failure. Rachel dropped me off at the bus depot; I called my mother, who picked me up at the Des Moines bus depot, at midnight.

"You'll never get me to do this again," she remarked when I got in. She was pointing over the steering wheel at the bums and drifters hanging around the parking lot.

Yet she was joking. I couldn't help but notice that she seemed (while feign-ing a certain commiseration) relieved.

Everything was called off. Rachel phoned me at work a few days later, plead-ing that she had made a terrible mistake. It was not a mistake, I told her:

"Rachel, was it really love this time? I think that after all these years we should finally give up and just try to be friends."

Rachel hung up on me.

Off I flew for Europe.

These incidents had preceded Rachel's letter, when it arrived in Hamburg seven months later. At the time I was living in a student dormitory—in a small, narrow room (six square meters), with a closet just to the right of the door, a single bed to the left and, at the end, a desk in front of a window.

My first problem was where Rachel was going to sleep. On the single bed, with me? We had never slept together before; I felt no desire to sleep with her now. I spoke to the tall, stern Hausleiterin, a black-haired woman with gray-blue eyes. There were no rooms available in the dormitory for at least a month.

"It is forbidden for a person to sleep in your room without this person being registered," she added. "There are extra charges."

Rachel and I had always kept our caresses relatively chaste, our more ardent adventures having been reserved for others. It was the emblem of our relationship. Not that the question had not arisen, even often, between us, especially after that first year of college when, after I had returned to Des Moines for the summer, Rachel and I had started going out again. But she would say, when I got carried away:

"Ours is real love. I don't want sex to become too important to us."

She sometimes spoke of the young man who had initiated her—I had not been initiated—a rock musician who had dropped out of Iowa State University, where she was a student. She had gone out with him for several months. I listened to her stories with fascination and even some terror, especially when she described the pain she had felt the first few times. As to us, we confined ourselves to what we called "embellishments."

On the day of Rachel's arrival in Hamburg, I arrived at the Bahnhof at least an hour ahead of time. (Strangely, while wandering around the station, I came across Françoise, walking towards a train, lugging a large gray suitcase. She was returning to Paris to see her professor. "I hope you'll find some time for me soon," I remarked in German, our common language back then, asking her how the master's thesis was coming along.)

Rachel had not so much as stepped off the train from Luxembourg when I felt her presence as an unbearable burden. She threw her arms around me, kissed me on the lips, as if nothing had changed. But everything had changed. I gave her an amicable hug, the best I could do.

During that first night of her visit I slept on the floor. It was an atrocious night that we both went through, Rachel begging me, till the wee hours of the morning, to climb into bed with her, while I tossed and turned on the linoleum floor, enveloped in a sleeping back—a hand's touch away. Remembering her own words, I said two or three times:

"If we are going to try to love each other again, then I don't want sex to be the reason."

After that, I had Rachel sleep in the apartment that Jon was renting, not far down the street, where there was a separate room and a separate bed. That expedient, I admit, was rather cruel.

Why recall all the sad details of her stay? We visited as many city sights as I could find, from museums followed by Konditoreien to a boat tour of the harbor and a stroll through the Reeperbahn red-light district at midnight. We got up at dawn to see the famous banana man at the market. We browsed for used books, even went to the top of the Fernsehnturm. We also took a three-day trip through Schleswig-Holstein, which concluded in a violent argument in a youth hostel at one o'clock in the morning.

On Rachel's last night in Hamburg—her last chance, and she still had not given up hope—I had us tag along with a group of German and American students who were heading downtown to a Greek tavern. On our way to the Othmarschen S-Bahn station, Jane—or was it Jean?—asked how my novel was coming along. Rachel looked at me with surprise; then she burst out laughing. I hardly spoke to her for the rest of the evening. The next morning I accompanied her to the Bahnhof, put her on the train to Barcelona. We never spoke nor wrote to each other again. I forwarded a few letters; from my parents (three years later) I learned that she had stayed on in Barcelona for several months, teaching English in a private school for Spanish businessmen.

There had always been a tacit agreement between us, even as early as our ninth-grade year at Franklin Junior High—when we had first met—that Rachel would be the writer and I—well, what exactly would I be? Not a writer in any case, although as I lost interest in sports and began reading more and more—two years later, the two of us now attending different high schools—Rachel and I would often talk about the books we had read; and sometimes we read them together. Once, after a few chapters, one of us had abandoned something by Sinclair Lewis, and I remember that while driving around the poorer parts of the city (as we would do, accurately imagining ourselves to be the only two inhabitants who knew Des Moines like the back of their hands) we discussed whether a reader, having begun a book, owed it to the author to read all the way to the end. We did not agree for a painful moment, but which of us then thought what? I no longer remember. In any case, I always came around to Rachel's point of view: the keenness of her mind was devastating, but that was not the main reason. My feelings for her were simply too strong (and at the same time too fragile); I feared that something as insignificant as a personal opinion would become an obstacle for her affection. I now wonder whether most of the time I really cared, while with Rachel, about trying to be my own person. Did the idea that a companion can help—or hinder—one to be, to become, oneself, even occur to me? And did I really care about the type of person Rachel might have been trying to become? I sincerely wanted to love her, but perhaps even more so wanted to be loved. Was it love that we—I for her, she for me—actually felt for each other? What was it that bound us together so strongly, and for such a long time?

Rachel was already, by the ninth grade, an accomplished writer. I do not remember how many prizes she had won by then. She was always entering stories in contests sponsored by magazines for teenagers, winning a few times and usually coming in at least third or fourth. Sometimes she showed me the stories, which back then were tender and symbolic, resembling O. Henry's "Gift of the Magi" and the like—with, however, more incisive characterization and more precise diction. In high school she was influenced by Hemingway; in college, it was Virginia Woolf. Early on she read the Brontë sisters, then George Eliot, then Jane Austen, then Henry James. She had read *Remembrance of Things Past* in its entirety. Rachel had an extraordinary vocabulary; she actually looked up in the dictionary the meanings of all the unknown words that she encountered.

I have rarely been able to take the first step towards those to whom, for whatever reason, I have been naturally attracted. When, at the age of fourteen, I noticed Rachel in Latin class, she proved to be no exception to this rule. In the fall of that year, it was she who invited me to the Snow Queen Dance, scheduled for December, three months later. It is true: it was a dance for which girls were supposed to ask boys, and they reserved us at least three months in advance. But usually a girl knew which boy(s) desired to be invited by her; the boy(s) would give at least one sign, usually many more. I had noticed Rachel, begun observing her: her large dark-brown eyes, her waist-length black hair, her rather assertive jaw which, it now strikes me, both intimidated me and made me feel protected. I listened carefully to her answers in class—to her voice. But I had neither said a word nor made the slightest gesture. Of course, Rachel had seen through me by then, anyway. In subsequent years, I often had the impression that she knew me better than I knew myself.

One October morning, in the hallway during the passing period after Latin class, Rachel invited me to the dance. She strode up to me, asked me abruptly, but at the same time in a soft, melodious tone that made me shudder, then, and thereafter, whenever I managed to recall the tone exactly. Above all, I was surprised, impressed, indeed charmed by what I later came to know well as one of her most telltale qualities: she could suddenly become incredibly bold, taking the most unbelievable risks, such as when (during her Hemingway period) she volunteered for a three-day course in bullfighting, during that trip to Spain which she took after graduating from high school.

Began the first and happiest period of our relationship: our meetings in the morning before homeroom; our one-minute meetings between classes (my galloping up the stairs to see her after biology class, my galloping back down to arrive on time in history class); our smiles and glances at each other during Latin (thwarted by gentle Mrs. Brinkmann: my attempt to swap assigned seats with Dan Cooney, who sat next to Rachel); our timid fingers touching for the first time at a Cinema Club movie (starring Tony Curtis); our holding hands while walking home after school (up 48th Street past Glendale Cemetery, down Forest Avenue to 45th); our long talks in the tiny kitchen of her house (Rachel serving me up a bottle of strawberry pop); our clumsy attempts to dance at the Snow Queen Dance (the fact that it didn't matter: neither of us liked dancing); our meetings on Sunday afternoons at the Northwest Branch of the Public Library; our first excursion, all by ourselves, to downtown Des Moines one Saturday afternoon (my father having dropped us off, Rachel's father having picked us up); our excursion to Omaha four years later (my own speeding ticket on the way back); our drives to Iowa City to find poetry books at the University Book Store; our stopping the car to kiss, one Saturday night, on a deserted country road near Perry, and the highway patrolman who suddenly drove up, got out, knocked on the driver's window (we hadn't even heard him), telling us to move on but at the same time suggesting a better spot . . . .

His unexpected final words:

"Good luck to you both!"

∞

I stopped reminiscing, read one last article.

Rachel had written about a project to install a sculpture garden in Greenwood Park, where we had walked so often, under the oak trees, one summer.

Would we ever meet again? If we met, would Rachel and I be able to forget the difficult and unpleasant moments of our common past, to look at each other with tenderness only, remembering the most moving and endearing moments, so happy to have come across—after so many years and undoubtedly for the last time—a person with whom we had gone through so much during those crucial years, with whom we had shared so much affection?

I hoped so, if it ever happened; but how to be sure?

And with these thoughts I left the library, which was closing. I walked slowly through downtown Des Moines, taking last glances at familiar landmarks, estranged by so much that was new.

Finally I arrived at my rented car. Putting the key in the lock, I looked up at the insurance company at which my father had worked for forty years, before retiring and moving to San Francisco. I felt the urge to take a drive—but to where? Through the neighborhoods in which Rachel and I had grown up? Past Franklin Junior High, now a fundamentalist church? To my mother's grave in Glendale Cemetery? I removed the key from the lock, turned, walked back to the hotel. Early the next morning my plane left for Europe.

The Driver's License

I had spent entire days trying to get my Iowa driver's license honored by the authorities at the local Prefecture when at last I gave up, took a last look at my bank account, signed up for driving lessons. We had moved from Paris to the provinces, we had bought a car. I needed a license. Françoise had found a school located not far from our apartment.

"Would you like to pay for your lessons separately?" asked the young woman in the entryway who, as I learned, was not the secretary of the school but the owner, Mme Georges. "Or would you prefer our special *forfait*."

As I hesitated to reply, she slowly passed the fingertips of her left hand through her frizzy, dyed-red hair. Her complexion was pasty, her face featureless, somewhat bloated. She was staring at me, with an indifference that seemed almost insolent.

"How much does a lesson cost?" I asked.

Behind us instructors came in, talking loudly, lighting cigarettes, reaching for various papers on the desk. It was ten o'clock. The first hour of lessons was over. Before answering my question Mme Georges asked one of the instructors:

"Can you work on Saturday morning again this week?"

The instructor smiled slyly, as if the question concealed an inside joke, while another instructor standing nearby, a thin elderly man with a narrow face, hurriedly touched the first one on the shoulder.

"I can if you can't!" he said with earnest.

But the first one rudely replied to the second one that he could.

Mme Georges turned back to us.

"A lesson costs 145 francs."

I glanced at Françoise, hoping she would make the necessary calculations. Despite a dozen years in France I still could not add mentally in the language, let alone multiply; each number I conjured up, envisioned before my eyes, before engaging in the slightest arithmetic operation. Even when buying fruit and vegetables at the Saturday market I sometimes misunderstood the prices barked back at me, especially when they involved numbers like *soixante-treize*, *quatre-vingt-deux*, *quatre-vingt-quatorze*.

"How much does the *forfait* cost?" I asked.

"2200 francs for ten lessons; 3600 francs for twenty."

"He's driven since the age of fourteen," interjected Françoise. "He needs only two or three lessons."

More interruptions: a check to endorse, followed by two phone calls, then from the back of the school a young woman cried out:

"The slides need to be changed, Madame!"

Mme Georges got up, stepped over the Doberman Pinscher sleeping at her feet, disappeared for a moment.

Françoise and I looked at each other; I found nothing to say. My fate was sealed. I had already resigned myself to the way the world was turning, as I had done on so many other occasion, both tragic and banal.

"That's what all foreigners think," remarked Mme Georges when she returned, stepping over the Doberman, taking her seat, imperturbably picking up the conversation where we had left it. "We've had other Americans go through the school. The minimum number of lessons is usually ten; twenty would be better. Otherwise you'll never pass. The French driving test is very difficult."

"Je suis Française," observed Françoise.

"Ah bon," replied Mme Georges.

In a moment she added:

"With the *forfait* our registration fees are waived, no matter how many times you fail the driving test."

She let us ponder this advantage, then continued:

"Of course, every time you fail—whether it be the written exam or the driving test—you'll have to buy new fiscal stamps."

"And how much do the fiscal stamps come to?"

"250 francs."

"If I understand correctly," I remarked, "if I decide not to take the *forfait* and if I fail either the written exam or the driving test, then I have to sign up at your school all over again."

"That's right," replied Mme Georges with a smile indicating that I should definitely opt for the *forfait*.

The elderly instructor was listening in. His thin pale face expressed worry, but also curiosity. I caught a whiff of his odor: lavender water; also that sweating, burnt smell—burnt leaves? burnt charcoal?—that emanates from certain synthetic fabrics.

His presence annoyed Mme Georges. With a glance and a nod towards the street she sent him to his next pupil. As he was glumly walking out the door I noticed his slumped shoulders. Was he to be my instructor?

"How much do the registration fees cost?" I asked.

"Our *frais de dossier* are 250 francs."

"Plus the fiscal stamps," I added.

"Plus the fiscal stamps."

"Did you say," I continued, "that if I take the *forfait* and if I fail the test, I still have to buy new fiscal stamps?"

"Yes, of course. It's French law, Monsieur. On the other hand, the new *frais de dossier* are waived."

"Of course."

"Not to mention that with the *forfait* you are entitled to an *écoute pédagogique*."

"An *écoute pédagogique*?"

The *écoute pédagogique* means that you can ask the instructor questions at the end of each lesson. He'll give you advice."

I immediately imagined, felt physically, the strange, austere silence of the lessons to come: the enclosed microcosm of the stuffy automobile, I concentrating on the road ahead, the instructor at my side studying the same road and occasionally observing my dexterity at the stick shift, with not a word exchanged between us since it was permissible to ask questions only at the end of each lesson. It would not at all be like my driver's education classes in high school, twenty years before, with jolly Mr. Peterson, an enormous gray-suited man who was always trying to pair up the boys and the girls obliged to ride with him. One spring morning the rumor spread that Mr. Peterson had touched Diane Flemming's sleeveless shoulder, that she had shuddered, that this was the real cause of her accident at the corner of Beaver Drive and Douglas Avenue.

"In other words," I remarked, "if I don't take the *forfait*, then I can't ask any questions at all?"

"We are very busy at our school," explained Mme Georges.

It is true that, except for the elderly instructor, the others had rushed in, rushed back out.

"Thus, if I take the *forfait*, they'll have time to answer my questions?" I wondered aloud.

"They'll make time," Mme Georges replied firmly.

That noon—for I still had not decided what to do—Françoise concluded that it was best to take the *forfait*.

"The problem," she explained, setting down on the kitchen table her favorite dessert, a small blue bowl full of *fromage blanc* daubed with fresh cream and sprinkled lightly with brown sugar, "is that no one knows what you need to do to pass the driving test the first time through. People say that if you don't take a *forfait*, then the inspectors will fail you automatically. They work hand-in-hand with the driving schools, probably take a cut for each student they test. In a town like Angers, everyone knows everyone, you can count on that."

"And if I waited until next fall?"

That afternoon, when I signed up for the *forfait*, I learned that I would benefit as well from a certain flexibility in the scheduling of the lessons. I asked if it would be possible to begin soon, indeed the next morning.

"Of course," replied Mme Georges. "We'll just cancel Mlle Raymond's appointment for tomorrow at ten."

I watched Mme Georges pick up the receiver, run the polished nail of her index finger down a computer listing, begin to dial. She put her hand over the mouthpiece.

"Her parents insisted on signing her up for only five lessons," she remarked, raising her eyebrows.

The next morning I met my instructor, Claude, a bearded man about my age—thirty-five. Or perhaps he was younger. He was short, stout, wore blue tennis shoes, baggy jeans and a faded checkered shirt. His shirttails hung out and between them I could see (as he walked towards me) his gaping, hirsute navel.

He was a chain-smoker.

My first lesson took place in the countryside, on the winding roads around La Meignanne and Saint-Lambert-la-Potherie. Small plots of farmland, a village or two, here and there a compact housing development; driving too quickly to notice more, I practiced shifting gears. It was the month of May and the weeds had already grown tall along the high banks of the roads. Indeed, some of the roads were nearly *chemins creux*, "sunken lanes"; there was little visibility. Claude encouraged me to try all the gears. Once or twice a tractor pulled out in front of us; then an old lady riding a bicycle—to whom I came rushing up while rounding a blind curve—forced me to brake sharply.

It was then that Claude, who had pressed hard on his instructor's brakes as well, stated sentessiously the first principle of French driving:

"*Vite quand on peut, lentement quand on doit.*" ("Drive fast if you can, slowly if you have to.")

During the *écoute pédagogique*, Claude told me that it was unlikely that I would pass the driving test the first time through.

"Why not?" I asked him.

"Ten lessons are not enough," he replied. "And you don't drive fast enough."

After a depressing lunch during which Françoise tried to bolster my morale by insisting that my instructor ("cet imbécile," she said) was only badgering me so that I would sign up for more lessons, I returned to the school and spent the entire afternoon watching slides in preparation for the written exam two weeks later. The practice exams were included in the *forfait*.

("A practice exam is *gratuit*," Mme Georges had explained. "You can come as often as you want.")

As in the real exam, true-to-life driving situations were flashed on the screen and the pupil had a few seconds in which to answer the multiple-choice question accompanying them. The question appeared—printed—on the slide, but was also announced by a taped voice, alternately male or female. The pupil, the viewer of the slide, was considered to be in the driver's seat. On the slide a car might be in front, the visibility good or bad, the road rise, dip or bend; it was important to look in the rearview mirror (always visible in the upper part of the slide), as well as at the painted lines on the roadway. Sometimes the speedometer was visible; it had to be read as well. "Should the car in front be passed?" Upon some minor detail the answer would depend.

In order to obtain the correct answers to the questions, the driver's manual had to be learned by heart. Mine cost 66 francs (not included in the *forfait*) and had 352 pages. Board games, sample tests, exercise books, coloring books, even shirts and T-shirts were available from the publisher of the driver's manual and sold at the school. But during the three weeks that I spent there, I never saw anyone wearing the shirts or T-shirts (or filling in the coloring books). The instructors dressed casually, though the thin elderly man did wear a tie. Pupils showed up in the latest teenage fashions, ready-to-wears made by popular mass-market designers. Mme Georges was a flashy dresser and obviously bought her clothes, if not in Paris, then in Nantes. She especially liked to wear her camel-colored leather pants during the cool mornings, but, after lunch, she would appear in something cottony, much lighter.

The intricacy of the driving laws was frightening. Great emphasis was placed on intriguing nuances, such as the rule that one yielded to hospital, but not to private ambulances at intersections. The difference between *stationnement* ("parking") and *arrêt* ("stopping" or "temporary parking") led to several distinctions (e.g., temporary double parking was permitted, as was temporary parking in front of someone's driveway), each of which in turn produced more distinctions, between "abusive," "dangerous" and merely "bothersome" parking or temporary parking, while dozens of specifically described infractions within these three categories could induce (depending on still more distinctions) the levying of a variety of fines and prison sentences. I particularly savored the question of priority on one-lane mountain roads: cars going uphill or downhill were to back up whenever encountering trailers, trucks or buses; trucks or buses going uphill or downhill were to back up for trailers.

"But who has the priority here, when a truck going downhill meets a bus?" I asked Mme Georges, calling her over to a slide.

"Common sense dictates the correct answer," she replied professorially, then returned to the desk, stepped over the Doberman, slid into her seat, became absorbed anew in her bookkeeping.

When no clients were negotiating their *frais de dossier* and no instructors were running about during their breaks, a monastic atmosphere reigned in the driving school. It was a meditative silence punctuated regularly only by the click of each new slide and the corresponding voice of the tape.

Simply memorizing the driver's manual by no means guaranteed that the pupil would pass the written exam: an entirely new way of looking at the world had to be assimilated. By studying the slides and reflecting on my many incorrect answers, slowly but surely I understood that, however dangerous the situation appeared, if French law theoretically permitted some act (e.g., passing, changing lanes), then the act not only could but should be carried out.

Thus a car in front should be passed at a railroad crossing (if the crossing had been supplied with gates or cross arms which functioned automatically) or at an intersection (if it was regulated by stoplights). Though at an unmarked intersection it was illegal to pass another car, it was legal to pass a motorcycle since, as the author of the manual contended, "a two-wheeled vehicle will not conceal a vehicle which is arriving from the right." On one type of roundabout the car entering had priority; on another type, the car entering was expected to yield. The most dangerous of all driving situations occurred whenever entering or leaving a *voie d'entrecroisement*. Found along urban expressways, *voies d'entrecroisement* were at once exits and entrances to expressways. *Voies d'entrecroisement* were safest during traffic jams, for otherwise cars crisscrossed at 80 km/h (=50 mph), even at 100 km/h (= 62 mph). Who had the priority on a *voie d'entrecroisement*? Who was supposed to yield? The cars leaving the expressway or those entering it? As the driver's manual put it, "There is no legislation on this matter, so the driver must be doubly careful."

Given the number of laws to learn, it surprised me that the teenagers with whom I sat practicing for the written exam were hardly studious at all. Some did not bother to answer any of the questions. Others cheated. One slept. Another, a young man aged slightly over twenty (which perhaps meant he had been failing the written test for over two years), drew obscene pictures on a large poster on the wall next to him, whenever Mme Georges was busy at her desk. The poster depicted the over hundred different traffic signs.

Thus arrows became penises, especially arrows indicating that a left or right turn was illegal. Road bumps became breasts. Falling rocks became fuming feces. Erections appeared on deer sprinting across the road. On my favorite, a triangular sign used for one type of roundabout and displaying the message "Vous n'avez pas la priorité," the three arrows chasing each other in a circle became penises, while the "n," the apostrophe and the "pas" of the message were crossed out, leaving: "Vous avez la priorité," "You have the priority."

Sometimes the young man would turn and give me a look so demented that I worried what he would be like on the road, a license in his pocket and a steering wheel in his hand.

I have always been shy in groups, so I spoke little to my fellow pupils. Moreover, I was ten to fifteen years older than nearly all of them. However, despite the difference in age, most of them addressed me with the *tu* instead of the *vous*, a linguistic act symbolizing our solidarity, each and every one of us equal before the difficulties of obtaining a license. Mme Georges, as well as the other instructors, also used the *tu* when speaking to us, although this symbolized something else for them, doubtless our condition, not as equals, but as pupils, as members of an inferior class: those who cannot yet drive a car. Little did it matter to Claude and Mme Georges that in fact I knew how to drive and had had a driver's license for twenty years. American driver's licenses, because of the low speed limits, because they would be obtained on automatic cars, were considered insufficient and even, by instructors such as Claude, somehow unmanly.

"The American licenses," he observed, "are not *sérieux*."

Of my comrades I did befriend a Togolese boy, Francis, who was a student at the agricultural high school. While Mme Georges changed the slides we talked about life in Angers, whether it was true that Angevins kept their doors closed to strangers, not to mention foreigners.

"Are there many Africans in Angers?" I asked him. "I must say I haven't seen many."

Francis shook his head, saying that he missed life in Paris, where he had lived for a few years with his brother.

"Where does your brother live in Paris?" I asked.

"In the thirteenth."

"That's my old arrondissement!" I exclaimed. "I miss Paris too."

Comparing addresses, we realized that we had lived only a few hundred meters apart. Perhaps Francis and his brother had been among the Africans who, every Sunday morning, played soccer on the abandoned tennis court located between the rue du Château-des-Rentiers and the rue Albert-Bayet. Returning from the bakery, a *boule de campagne* in my hand, I had often lingered to watch them, secretly desiring to join in. One day Francis came no more. I learned from Mme Georges that he had passed both the written exam and the driving test the first time through. I never saw him again. Did he ever pass, as he had hoped, the difficult entrance exam to that landscape architecture school in Versailles?

After my first lesson in the countryside, my remaining nine lessons took place in the two suburban parts of town in which the driving tests took place: Belle-Beille and La Roseraie. In the former was situated the university at which Françoise had been given a teaching job; in the latter lived several of her colleagues. Both suburbs had their full share of high-rise, low-cost apartment buildings, not to mention scores of prefabricated houses, all exactly alike from roof to wine cellar, most of them neatly arranged around squares and circles or along winding streets. The official name of La Roseraie was "ZUP-Sud" or "Zone à Urbaniser en Priorité", and it was this name that was used by Angevins desiring to disparage the area, and particularly by those who lived the reputably more elegant area around the Catholic University, located not all that far from La Roseraie. La Roseraie was located in the southern part of the city, Belle-Beille to the north.

During the second or third écoute pédagogique Claude explained that if I were to pass the test (which he still thought unlikely), then I would have to know all the *pièges* of Belle-Beille and La Roseraie. That is, the traps and tricky places: the one-way streets, the dead ends, the roundabouts, the legal and illegal turns, above all the unmarked intersections at which the driver was expected to slow down and, if necessary, yield to cars coming perpendicularly from the right and sometimes even obliquely from the right, blindly, from behind. We had moved to Angers only a few months before and knew the local streets only by bus and by foot. What pedestrian cares if a street is one- or two-way? What bus rider pays attention to bus lanes that appear and disappear, to right turns that buses and taxis can take but not cars? During every lesson, Claude and I would go over one or two of the *circuits*, the itineraries (full of tricky places) that the inspectors typically chose for the tests.

"Drive around her with your wife after our lesson," Claude would warn. "It is neither our problem nor the inspector's that you haven't mastered the layout of the streets."

During a lesson, whenever I was faced with a barrage of one-way streets, blocked-off roads and no-left-turn signs, he would test me:

"Turn to the left as soon as you can."

It was apparently a command that inspectors often gave.

After five or six lessons Mme Georges learned from the authorities at the Prefecture that my test would take place in La Roseraie.

"I have my ways of finding out," she remarked.

"Do you think I'll pass?" I asked.

She put out her hand, palm down, flattened it, spread out her fingers, turning her wrist so that the thumb, then the little finger, moved successively up and down.

"Your instructor says it will be very touch-and-go," she replied.

Thereafter, Claude and I practiced exclusively on the *circuits* in La Roseraie.

La Roseraie and Belle-Beille had been chosen by the inspectors of the Prefecture since these two suburban areas offered the greatest variety of types of streets. In La Roseraie there were busy boulevards leading to and from the *rocade*, the city expressway. Streets went by schools and shopping centers. There were dead ends and confusingly marked roundabouts, narrow one-way streets and, near the Maine River, what nearly were country roads. There were parking lots, places to parallel park, places to park side-by-side, also places that looked like places to park but which—if one read the street signs correctly— were not. In the southernmost part of La Roseraie quiet streets wound gently through new housing developments—streets which bore, like the district itself, romantic names such as the rue du Buis, the rue du Liseron or the rue de la Lavande. Claude would often have me drive, just south of La Roseraie, along the chemin haut de la Baumette. During the daytime I noticed nothing, but one evening weeks later, walking with Françoise and two young friends along the right bank of the Maine River, near the village of Bouchemaine and across the river from the chemin haut de la Baumette, I saw a line of slow-moving headlights, a sort of procession.

"They're looking over the prostitutes," explained our friends, who (like Francis) had gone to the agricultural high school not far from there.

All the *circuits* in La Roseraie began at the Jardin de la Roseraie, the garden for which the area had been named.

"This is where you'll wait to take your test," observed Claude, slowing the car suddenly with his instructor's brakes, a disorienting change in speed that always gave me nausea.

He was pointing to the rows of rosebushes coming into bloom.

"Do you like roses?" I asked.

I was thinking of the dozens of rose gardens through which I had strolled during my lifetime and of my indifference to, and on some afternoons vehement dislike of, hybrids, no matter how spectacular their hues and perfect their forms.

"Yes," replied Claude.

"And if he asks you to head south from here," he continued, "down the avenue Maurice-Tardat, that usually means you'll have to do one or two *manoeuvres* before going out to the expressway."

By *manoeuvres* Claude meant parallel parking, backing up into a confined space or turning completely around at the end of a narrow dead-end street with neither driveways nor a circle at the end. For the latter, the "three-point turn," he taught a refined technique of which he was very proud. Thus, approaching the end of the street, the pupil would be taught to slow down, to shift into first, to turn the steering wheel to the left as far as it would go while keeping the car advancing ever so slowly—by delicate footwork on the clutch and accelerator—until, at the very last instant before the front wheels touched the far curb, he would give two rapid, complete turns of the steering wheel to the right.

The turning back of the steering wheel at the last instant straightened the wheels and facilitated the second step of the three-point turn.

For now, with the front wheels resting on the far curb—a natural brake which kept a car with manual transmission from rolling forward—the driver could shift into reverse, turn the steering wheel as far to the right as it would go while ever so slowly backing up until, at the very last instant before the back wheels touched the first curb, he would give (as before) two rapid, complete turns of the wheel to left.

Whereupon, the back wheels now resting on the curb, the car could be put into first gear again and—as the driver turned the steering wheel sharply to the left—be driven back down the street without grazing the tires on the far curb while pulling around.

Claude would take me to practice the three-point turn on a street so narrow that every centimeter counted if I were to avoid grazing the tires.

"If you graze them," he warned, "the inspector will ask you to do the *manoeuvre* all over again. If you graze your tires twice you fail the test."

"And have to buy new fiscal stamps?" I joked.

"And have to buy new fiscal stamps."

From his instructor's seat, Claude could perform any of the *manoeuvres*—including parallel parking—with an eye on the right side-view mirror and while steering with his left hand only.

Except for discussions of technical matters such as *manoeuvres* and potential tricky places—discussions few and far between for, after all, I was an experienced driver—Claude and I found little talk about. He asked few questions about my personal life; that I was an American living in a medium-sized town in the west of France impressed him little, if at all. Most of the time he seemed to be daydreaming, gazing at the vineyards near Épiré and Savennières or, if we had returned to La Roseraie, at the mothers walking their children home from school, at the delivery vans, at the dusty, dark-green hedges bordering the parking lots. He would bring his cigarette, held between his index and middle fingers, to his lips, puff on it slowly while squinting, then lower it until his hand rested on his knee; he would exhale the smoke forcibly against the inside of the windshield. The smoke whirled towards me, enveloped me.

My major problem was the speed at which I was expected to drive the car in the city. Back then, the law allowed up to 60 km/h (= 37 mph) on city streets, with (strangely, in comparison to the parking and temporary parking laws) no distinction made between wide avenues and narrow one-way side streets, between thoroughfares running alongside industrial areas and streets crossing school or hospital zones. Claude constantly urged me to shift into fourth gear.

"But I'm already going 55 (= 34 mph)," I would complain while racing down a narrow street lined on both sides with parked cars.

"Move up to 60 and shift into fourth."

I would accelerate to 60, shift into fourth, then (after a few seconds) instinctively take my foot from the pedal and shift back into third.

At the end, when Claude had lost patience with my *conduite molle*, with my "limp, lifeless, lethargic driving," he would sometimes, suddenly, push down hard on the instructor's accelerator. The car would speed forward amidst my cries of protest; once I shouted "Espèce d'idiot, laissez-moi tranquille!"; but Claude only laughed, his left hand gripping the steering wheel, his feet manipulating the instructor's pedals, bringing the car back within the speed limit. Then he would say, seriously:

"C'est toi, l'espèce d'idiot. If you don't learn how to drive fast you'll never get a license."

The written test was scheduled for a Tuesday at 1:15 p.m., at the Salle Saint-Laud. It was a dusty old theater, located just behind the Église Saint-Laud, and still used for amateur productions—a theater with several broken seats, with a faded carpet running down the aisles, a carpet that in places (because of missing tacks) had bunched into little folds upon which unheeding spectators inevitably caught the toes of their shoes and tripped. We had attended a few cultural evenings there: a reading of odes and sonnets penned by a pretentious local poet; a student production, in German, of Lessing's *Minna von Barnhelm*; and other plays that I no longer remember. Françoise postponed a meeting at the university in order to accompany me to the test.

As when taking a train and though the theater was only a five-minute walk from our apartment, I insisted that we arrive at least a half-hour ahead of time. Françoise suggested that a half-hour was excessive, that I would become more nervous waiting outside the theater for the doors to open than if I arrived, "bien reposé," right on time. Nonetheless, observing me, she acquiesced. By 12:30 we were sitting on the steps of the church.

In about fifteen minutes I did consent to a short walk. On the rue du Temple I curiously recalled a trip to Germany, perhaps because of the post-World-War-II architecture of the apartment buildings on that street, perhaps because of the cold shadows—the proverbial "coldness" of Germany—reminiscent of ten chilly February days spent in Frankfurt a few years before.

The other candidates started showing up five or six minutes before one o'clock. Among them was a girl next to whom I had often sat—in the dark at the school—watching slides. I had even exchanged several words with her. But when I said hello she looked at me strangely, wondering who I was.

"At the school, she never seems to make mistakes on the practice exams," I remarked to Françoise.

In a few minutes I left Françoise and joined the crowd waiting for the doors to open. There were at least a hundred people waiting there: for the most part, students from the lycées and the two universities, but also middle-aged men and women forced, probably because of convictions for driving while intoxicated, to take the written test again. Not to forget the friends and spouses accompanying the candidates, and the representatives (in our case, Mme Georges herself) of every driving school in town.

When the doors finally opened, at exactly 1:15, the representatives were required, one after another, to "present" their candidates to the inspector in charge of conducting the written exam. One by one, in the foyer of the theater, our names were called out. We each stepped forward. The inspector compared the spelling of the name on his list to the one on Mme Georges' list, then examined the fiscal stamps on our inscription forms. One by one, we were given permission to enter the theater, but we were also told to remain in line at the back, in the precise order in which we had initially been called. No one said a word.

In a moment (for ours had been the last school to present its candidates), the inspector entered the theater, walked past us down the aisle, climbed the steps to the stage and set up a screen, came back down, walked to one of the center rows and set up a slide projector, then a tape recorder. He turned on the projector, adjusted the light, slipped in a sample slide and focused the lens. Then he shut off the projector and removed the slide. He tested the tape recorder. Finally he walked back towards the stage. He sat down, slightly to the right of the stage, at a table upon which a quaint porcelain desk lamp had been placed. Strangely, I had the impression that the inspector had brought the porcelain lamp from his own living room.

Once again he called us forward one by one. Taking the identity card or foreign permit in hand, he examined it under the harsh light, twisting the card slightly to remove the reflecting glare of the plastic covering. He scrutinized the candidate's face. After checking the identity card, the inspector told the candidate to take his or her seat, stipulating that a place be left vacant on both adjoining sides. Depending on the number of candidates, each school was allotted a row, or two, or three; when all the candidates from a school were seated, a new row was begun for the next school. The five or six of us from

Mme Georges' school were finally given permission to take our seats, towards the back of the theater.

To each candidate the inspector gave an answer form, an oblong computer card kept in place in a specially designed plastic holder. Then he gave us the "stylus" used for perforating the card. The inspector's directions concerning the perforating of the cards took quite some time. At the top of the form I filled in my name, address, date of birth, sex. An optional question requested the candidate's profession, and for an instant I toyed with the idea of taking advantage of this slight liberty. Finally I marked the appropriate box: "Other."

Then the inspector turned on the projector, the tape recorder, and we answered four sample questions. As in the practice sessions at the school (in the end Mme Georges had given us similar answer forms and styluses), a slide was flashed on the screen while we read the possible answers to the multiple-choice question and listened to them repeated by a taped voice. When a few seconds had gone by, the next slide appeared. I immediately noticed that the sample questions included only two or three, instead of four possible answers, and that we had more time in which to answer them than during the practice exams at the school. The inspector turned off the projector. He asked if we had all understood what we were supposed to do.

We all had, it seemed.

He turned the projector back on and the test began.

Of the forty slides only two or three gave me trouble. One showed a car parked halfway off a flat, unshouldered *route départementale* (or secondary "departmental highway") and inquired whether the car was legally parked; another depicted one of the two green arrows (especially important during the holidays and their notorious traffic jams) indicating an *itinéraire bis* or "alternate route" either to or from Paris. The arrow was not completely filled in: the center was white, the lines forming the arrow were green. Did this mean that the alternative route was heading towards Paris? Or from Paris to the provinces? I couldn't remember. My chances were fifty-fifty.

I was grateful that no questions were about the "discontinuous" or "broken" white lines painted on the roadways. Depending on the type of road or intersection, six main kinds of discontinuous painted lines could appear:

Type 1:   a 3-meter line separated by a 10-meter interval
Type 1A: a 1.5-meter line separated by a 5-meter interval
Type 2:   a 3-meter line separated by a 3.5-meter interval

Type 2A: a 0.5-meter line separated by a 0.5-meter interval
Type 3:   a 3-meter line separated y a 1.33-meter interval
Type 3A: a 20-meter line separated by a 6-meter interval

But the distinctions did not end here: the width of the discontinuous painted line also needed to be taken into account. The candidate might otherwise misinterpret, in the limited perspective offered by the slide, the type of broken line (to the left, to the right, or both) that his car was running alongside; he might answer the question in a way that implied that he was crossing the line(s) illegally. In order to calculate the correct width, the following variable was employed:

u = 7.5 centimeters for tollways and urban expressways
u = 6 centimeters for national and departmental highways
u = 5 centimeters for all other roads

Thus, taking a simple case, such as when a discontinuous line indicated an emergency parking lane—a line falling into the Type 3A category—then the width of the line was indicated in the manual as being "3 x u"; in other words, 22.5 centimeters for emergency parking lanes located on tollways and expressways; 18 centimeters for emergency parking lanes located on national and departmental highways; and 15 centimeters for emergency parking lanes located on any other kind of road.

Theoretically, there were many other types of roads on which broken lines were found and which, during the exam, might call for further calculations. There were other widths and thus more formulas to keep in mind. For example, the formula used for calculating the width of the broken line (in the Type 2 category) indicating a *voie d'entrecroisement* was "5 x u"; in other words, 37.5 centimeters for tollways and urban expressways; 30 centimeters for national and departmental highways; and 25 centimeters for *voies d'entrecroisement* located on any other kind of road. It was not likely, of course, that a *voie d'entrecroisement* would be found on roads other than urban expressways, but one had to be prepared for every possibility.

It was interesting that the width of the simplest kind of broken line—the line dividing lanes on roads located either outside or inside the city limits (lanes respectively in the Type 1 and Type 1A categories)—increased when the road approached a traffic island. The formula changed (in both cases) from "2 x u" to "3 x u". Thus, for a national highway running either outside or inside the city limits, the width changed from 12 to 18 centimeters as the highway approached a traffic island. Though the widths remained the same, the lengths of the broken lines and the corresponding intervals between them naturally changed when the highway left the city limits: leaving the Type 1A category (1.5-meter lines, 5-meter intervals), the highway entered the Type 1 category (3-meter lines, 10-meter intervals).

The day before the test I had tried to memorize the formulas, but all the time hoped that the exam questions (or questions!) would simply appeal to the logic that I had discerned behind the many precise distinctions. One drove faster outside the city limits; thus, the lines were longer and the intervals between them greater. In addition, as the manual put it: "Plus il y a de peinture, plus il faut être vigilant" ("The more paint there is, the more careful one must be.") But this admirable maxim did not help the candidate examining the slide to count, in a few seconds, the number of intervals (or broken lines) located between his car and the one ahead, and thus to calculate whether the *distance de sécurité* was sufficient.

I had amply prepared myself by practicing on the slides at the school and thus felt quite sure that I could pass. Five errors were permitted. However, during the test, I began worrying whether I was correctly perforating the answer card. My stylus seemed blunt. While punching out the tiny holes (no more than two millimeters in width), I noticed that an infinitesimal corner of paper often covered a part of the hole of that the punched part had not fallen neatly into the plastic holder but remained dangling along the side. Scratching with the blunt stylus at the dangling bits of paper, I could not easily remove them so as to obtain a perfect hole. Would this affect the answers when the card passed through the computer?

Towards the end of the test the girl in front of me raised her hand. She had suddenly realized that her answers off by one, that instead of punching the slot for the first question she had punched the slot for the second question, and so on. The inspector's reaction startled me.

He shouted.

He shouted that he had explained how to punch the cards and that she would have to sign up for the test again.

The girl, in tears, stood up, stormed out of the theater, trying pathetically to slam one of the panels of the double door. The panel flapped back and forth, back and forth, back and forth—making a swishing sound.

We finished the test.

Once again we were called forward, one by one. It was easy to know who had passed: as the inspector let the card fall through an oblong box attached to the computer, the correct answers to any missed questions on a card having more than five errors were automatically printed out on a narrow band of paper; for cards with five errors or less, nothing was printed. Laughing broke out when one of the candidates—quite ostentatiously of the high-school hoodlum variety—stood by the computer for a very long time while the printer tick-tapped out about thirty correct answers. The inspector shouted again, muffling the laughter. I expected the high-school hoodlum to unroll the band of paper to arm's length, smile at the inspector with terrifying irony and then, with a flick of both wrists, snap the paper in two. I expected him to let it fall to the floor, then to saunter ever so slowly up the aisle, reaching for a pack of cigarettes that had been rolled up into the sleeve of his T-shirt. I expected him to turn back, to threaten the inspector by pointing to the tattoo on his biceps—a knife piercing a heart. But all this I imagined, including the pack of cigarettes rolled up into his sleeve and the ominous tattoo. Like the other candidates, the high-school hoodlum folded up the band of paper, put it into the back pocket of his jeans and quietly, sadly, even shamefully, left the theater.

My card fell through the box. I had missed two questions. I had passed! Françoise and I decided to celebrate the event with crêpes and cider in the tiny crêperie tucked away on the rue des Angles, an indeed angular street zigzagging behind the department store, Les Nouvelles Galeries.

First we sat down in the back room, a glass-enclosed porch-like construction, but later carried our *bolées de cidre* and crêpes back to the front room, once an elderly couple had sat down at the table alongside ours and the man had drawn from his shirt pocket a pack of the most pungent French cigarettes, those Gitanes rolled in a special yellow paper.

I had only an hour's worth of driving lessons left. My driving test was scheduled for three o'clock the next day. When I dropped by the school after our crêpes, Mme Georges informed me that I would be taking the final lesson, not with Claude, but with her husband.

"The best thing," she remarked, "would be for you to take the lesson from two to three, in other words just before the test. In that way you can practice with the same car you'll take the test in."

I was immediately alarmed that I would have to take the test in a car with an entirely different type of stick shift!

But I said nothing.

Then I asked:

"Now that I've had nine lessons, do you think I'll pass, Mme Georges?"

Mme Georges put out her hand, flattened it, spread out her fingers, turning the wrist so that the thumb, then the little finger, successively moved up and down. She shrugged her shoulders, pursed her lips. Her eyes bulged slightly with unknowingness.

"Just a moment," she said.

She examined the *planning*, an enormous sheet of paper with the week's driving lessons noted on it.

"Claude is free tomorrow from nine to eleven . . . ."

"Non, non, ça va," I remarked, and bade her good-bye.

As I was leaving she added:

"You can always drive around La Roseraie this evening with your wife. Maybe that will help. Whatever happens, drop by and see us after the test. Let's hope for the best."

When I arrived at the school the next day, M. Georges, whom I now recognized as that svelte, dandyish young man who fluttered about the school during the breaks (I had thought that he was a mere instructor), was waiting for me near a slightly newer version of the same Renault-5 model that I had been driving. Already sitting in the back seat was another candidate, who would be taking the test with me. He was about eighteen, somewhat pimply and, judging by the way he had brought his knees up to his chest, quite tall. I got in, turned and shook his hand—with difficulty because of the headrest. Then M. Georges got in. Off we went.

I edged into the line of cars moving down the rue d'Alsace. Everything was fine. I relaxed. I stopped to let several pedestrians stroll across the crosswalk near Les Nouvelles Galeries and pointed out to M. Georges that I was thereby respecting an admirable statute of the driving code, one requiring drivers to stop "if the pedestrian has taken at least one foot from the curb and set it down on the crosswalk."

"There is a limit to every law," retorted M. Georges, gesturing for me to drive ahead, through the crowd.

Then I drove around the place du Ralliement, the surprisingly small central square of a town which, according to tourist and Chamber of Commerce brochures, claimed over 200,000 inhabitants. I turned onto the rue de la Chaussée-Saint-Pierre, a stub of a street which nonetheless always struck me as Parisian, probably because the buildings on both sides of the street, seemingly taller than most of the others in the center of Angers (in fact they were not), blocked out the sun in the same way that Parisian buildings do. It was a street that pedestrians always hurried down, nowhere else in Angers so quickly bundling up their coats, re-knotting their scarves and feeling so anonymous—before they reached the warmth of the place du Ralliement.

Then came the first tricky intersection, the Carrefour Rameau. I had long rechristened it the "carrefour Maurice-Fourré (1876-1959)" in honor of a local writer, a precursor of the Surrealists, who by the end of his life had attained a national reputation—of very short duration. Composed of six streets, not four, the intersection was tilted obliquely so as to provide unusual perspectives in all directions.

I was on my habitual route out of town: up the rue Chaperonnière, past the place Sainte-Croix and its medieval Maison d'Adam, then up then down the rue Toussaint towards the Château. I often walked this way: the bookstore on the rue Chaperonnière, the pastry shop (with their *tartes grand-mère*) on the place Sainte-Croix, the public library at the bottom of the rue Toussaint. M. Georges indicated that he wanted to stop for gas and wash the car.

"We always try to make a good impression on the inspectors," he explained.

As for myself, I was wearing my lucky mustard-colored tie with its 18th-century fox-hunting scenes.

At the corner of the Château we turned right and headed down the boulevard du Général-de-Gaulle, towards the Maine River. The gas station was located on the other side of the pont de la Basse-Chaîne, in a quarter called La Doutre. Claude had often asked me to stop at the same station, telling me to keep the motor running while he went inside to buy a soft drink and a bag of chocolate-chip cookies. As Claude was waiting to pay, I would practice shifting into reverse, the Renault-5 stick-shift being uncomfortably stiff and requiring that the driver use two fingers to pull up hard on an underneath part of the stick-shift knob. It was not easy. As for the cookies, Claude would have eaten nearly all of them by the end of the hour. Not once did he offer me one, not once did I ask.

As M. Georges was paying for the gas and car wash, the other candidate and I talked about the upcoming test. He told me that he had already failed seven times!

"Once it was the three-point turn," he explained insolently. "Another time—I still don't know what happened—I ran the car up onto the curb of an expressway exit ramp."

"Really?"

"Then the last few times I have been accused of not driving fast enough. Oh yeah, I nearly forgot," he laughed. "Once I misread a sign and turned onto a narrow one-way street—the wrong way. The inspector had asked me to turn to the right as soon as possible. For some reason I thought the sign was for parking."

His laugh I will never forget. Not one of his failures had affected him in the slightest. I had recognized myself momentarily in this beardless, overgrown boy, but now remembered how obsessed with failure I had been at his age. He was apparently not obsessed. Was I still so obsessed?

Soon we arrived at La Roseraie. Several cars were already lined up along the avenue Maurice-Tardat, and waiting by the curb were two girls whom I recognized from the slide sessions at the school. M. Georges told us to get out and stand at some distance from the car. We walked over to the sidewalk, several meters away. M. Georges, however, got out and simply changed seats. Now he was sitting in the back, on the right-hand side.

Coming towards the car was the inspector from the day before!

Disregarding us, he opened the front right-hand door, took his seat. He did not shake M. Georges's hand, nor even look at him. After examining a sheaf of papers in his lap for several minutes, he turned, reached out, took from M. Georges's hand our examination forms. As the inspector studied the forms I could not help but notice the several fiscal stamps on the overgrown boy's form. They formed a dull red splotch.

One of the girls whispered:

"He's supposed to be fairly lenient."

"You should have seen him at the written exam yesterday," I replied.

"I haven't had that one yet," sneered the overgrown boy.

The girl shrugged her shoulders. The inspector rolled down the window and called us over to the car.

With a "Vous êtes Monsieur Taylor?" he designated me as the first candidate. M. Georges remained in the back; the overgrown boy got in beside him, on the other side. When I had settled myself behind the wheel, I buckled my seat belt, then meticulously adjusted the side mirror and the rearview mirror, as Claude had counseled me to do.

"Adjust it two or three times before you turn on the engine," he had suggested.

Then I took a pair of sunglasses from my shirt pocket.

This provoked the first sign of tension between me and the inspector.

I saw him searching for a detail on my papers, then he asked:

"Are those real glasses?"

"No, they are not," I replied, removing them so that he could see for himself.

"Leave them on," he commanded. "Ça va!"

But during the test he had me pull into a parking lot, stop, and read to him what was written on a distant billboard—at the bottom, underneath the illustrations of wicker couches and armchairs, in fine print and introduced by an asterisk: "Cette offre n'est valuable que pour les achats de 2000F ou plus." ("This offer applies only to purchases of at least 2000 francs.") When that gave me no difficulty he asked me to turn on the windshield wipers. Then to turn them off. To turn on the headlights; the bright lights. Then to dim them. Then to turn them off. Finally to turn on the heater.

He didn't say anything after that except that I should head off in a new direction. Side streets; several turns. I had no idea where we were until we came back to the boulevard Joseph-Bédier.

I drove for a while down that boulevard, which was not in fact a boulevard but rather a narrow avenue just wide enough for two lanes on each side. I maintained a safe position in the sluggishly moving right lane, at the end dodging a car that cut in front of me at the roundabout.

"Vous n'avez pas chaud?" asked the inspector sinisterly, after I had successfully negotiated the roundabout.

He turned to catch M. Georges's eye. M. Georges laughed.

I turned off the heater.

The inspector very much disliked, as Claude and M. Georges had predicted, my cautious driving. At the beginning of the test, as we were heading down the avenue Maurice-Tardat—the little Renault-5 gliding along almost as smoothly as my parents' Chevrolet, so many years before, on a shady avenue in my Midwestern hometown—the inspector remarked icily, without looking at me:

"I expect you to drive at all times at the speed limit. Unless it is absolutely impossible. I will not repeat this rule twice."

I immediately sped up to 60 km/h (= 37 mph) and gritted my teeth; when I swerved (not forgetting, however, to signal a lane change) to miss a pedestrian standing on the street side of his parked car, the inspector seemed pleased. Luckily, once I had turned off the avenue Maurice-Tardat onto the boulevard Robert d'Arbisel, a surprising amount of traffic for a Tuesday afternoon kept the speeds down to a comfortable 45 km/h (= 28 mph).

Everything went well, parallel parking included, until the inspector ordered me onto the *rocade*. I edged the car (over a treacherous *voie d'entrecroisement*) into the speeding traffic, pushed down on the accelerator until I had attained 90 km/h (= 56 mph), the limit for first-year drivers. Cars whizzed by at well over the regular limit, 110 km/h (= 69 mph). Nonetheless, I soon found myself coming up on a semi which, as I recalled from the manual, was not allowed to exceed 90. It was going slightly less than that.

I thought that the inspector would be impressed by a slightly exaggerated *distance de sécurité*, so I slowed slightly, to about 85 km/h (= 53 mph), leaving a good 40 meters between our car and the back of the semi. A few seconds went by. Then the inspector shouted, as he had done the day before at the girl who had mispunched her computer card. He shouted that he had already warned me about driving slowly!

Wondering what would become of me, indeed of us all, I sped back up to 90 kmh. This brought us to within one or two meters of the back of the semi. I could see nothing ahead of us, except two shiny steel doors with "Fruehauf" printed on each panel. I don't know how far we sped along like that, locked into a common destiny, an enormous semi delivering products to some far-off destination—Italy or Poland or wherever—and our driving-school Renault-5 enveloping ludicrously with flimsy metal four ill-fated companions for a smash-up, each of us disliking—perhaps hating—the others and conscious of *or was I the only one conscious of?* the unavoidable, indeed risible event that had yoked us together *for this absurd death* I was thinking as I concentrated on the back lights of the semi *would he turn? brake?* out of the corner of my left eye more cars whizzing by caught up in this vicious Necessitas the inspector not a word from the inspector as we pursued in the death race the semi heading for Poland the semi. . . .

The right tail light began blinking, I had noticed in time, I braked, gently, the semi turned off the *rocade*, I drove on to the next exit, the inspector ordered me off, I turned off, he finally told me to stop in a small parking lot nearby, on the boulevard Charles-Barangé. He told me to get out of the car, to change places with the beardless, overgrown boy.

When I slid in beside M. Georges he looked at me sadly, raising his eyebrows. Then he made the same gesture that his wife liked to make: he put out his hand, flattened it, spread out his fingers, turning his wrist so that his thumb, then his little fingers, successively moved up and down.

The tour that the overgrown boy gave us was wild. So fast and furiously did he drive that I forgot my previous fears while tailgating the semi and acquired new ones. The overgrown boy's strategy, since he had failed the test three times for "slow driving," was obviously to impress the inspector with sporty starts, quick turns and speedy lane-changes. These he performed with an aplomb oblivious to all surrounding dangers. I could not see the speed-ometer, but I was sure that he was driving at 5-10 km/h over the speed limit. The inspector remained imperturbable, his eyes fixed straight ahead. I noticed, just below his left sideburn, that he had nicked himself that morning while shaving.

Feeling the rising nausea of the helpless, imprisoned car passenger—tossed to and fro, fore and aft—I took refuge in that absurd, yet comparatively calm and immobile detail. I had once used a similar technique when crossing the English Channel by ferryboat. As the waves tossed the boat every which way, I stilled my nausea by speaking as rapidly as I could to a teenage girl sitting across from me; she also spoke rapidly, and I remember that we stared grimly and courageously into each other's eyes as well.

After successfully swerving his way onto, driving on, then exiting from the *rocade*—all of this at breakneck speed—the overgrown boy was asked to make a few turns, until we arrived at a small parking lot on the rue Gagarine, a quiet street surrounded by high-rise apartment buildings. Not a pedestrian was in sight. The inspector designated an unoccupied parking space, on only one side of which was a car, and ordered the overgrown boy to back into it.

I don't know why, but suddenly I felt nervous, as if I myself had been ordered to perform the *manoeuvre*. In a succession of uncontrollable images I relived many of my own past failures: my inability in kindergarten to run with the others after I had recovered from polio; my speechlessness when led, as the "honor-night speaker," to the podium in the Y-Camp lodge when I was seven or eight; in ninth grade my falling off the rope halfway up and my weightlifting all winter long so as to be able to climb to the gym rafters the next year; my numerous failures to stand up to all sorts of fellow human beings—parents, bosses, girlfriends, neighbors, civil servants, driving-school instructors, butchers. . . .

The overgrown boy stalled the motor, inexplicably, when the tires settled in a shallow gutter, one side of which formed a slight inclined plane leading up to the parking space.

The inspector asked him to try again.

What now happened was extraordinary.

As the overgrown boy restarted the engine, drove the car forward a few meters, shifted into reverse and began backing up in sudden jerks, M. Georges and I had the simultaneous impression that the boy was turning the wheel too far to the right. That is, evidently startled by the same perceptions of our surroundings, we both turned our heads at the same time to the right, looked over our shoulders at the left-hand side of the car parked in the next space— only centimeters away!

Again the boy was having a difficult time bringing the car out of the gutter, up and over the slight inclined plane. The car struggled upwards, then rolled back down. But the boy also kept turning the wheel to the right! I wanted to shout: "Look over you shoulder, idiot, you're going to run into another car!" But I said nothing, only glancing at the side of the inspector's stern face, at the nick below his sideburn. It was an exam, after all. Looking straight ahead, the inspector nonetheless had, I noticed, one sharp eye riveted on the side-view mirror to his right.

Just then the overgrown boy let out the clutch, we bolted backwards while instantaneously the inspector slammed down on his brakes—we bolted forwards. Turning once again to look over my shoulder, I saw that the right tail-light of our Renault-5 was no more than a centimeter from the back left side of the other car. I was sweating, so was M. Georges; the inspector shouted:

"Allez-y, dégagez, avancez!"

Not one word was spoken, between the rue Gagarine and the avenue Maurice-Tardat, except for the inspector's icy commands:

"À droite . . . à droite . . . tout droit . . . à droite. . . ."

Once we had pulled up in front of the Jardin de la Roseraie and parked, the inspector told me to get out of the car and wait "over there, near that tree."

He pointed to one of the poplars lining the ominously dark street.

I left the overgrown boy to his fate, worried enough about my own. The girl to whom I had spoken earlier and who was still waiting for her own test greeted me. In a daze, I hadn't even noticed her.

"You were the first to drive, weren't you?" she asked.

"Yes."

"Well, when they ask you to get out, that usually means the other fellow has failed the test and you haven't."

I had just enough time to mention my own doubts and evoke the overgrown boy's near-accident, when he got out of the car. He slammed the door, stormed off down the avenue.

"Go now," said the girl. "It's your turn. Good luck."

The inspector had not called me, but, yes, he was expecting me to get in and hear his verdict. He even seemed impatient, as if I had tarried. Besides my trepidation, besides my awe in regard to the entire experience I had just been through, I now felt marvel for the girl: she had known exactly what I was supposed to do. How many situations had arisen during my lifetime when I had no idea of what I was supposed to do, what I was supposed to say! How grateful I was whenever someone told me clearly!

"Ça peut aller," said the inspector, "your driving is passable."

I had passed!

From his hand I took the pink slip with which (as he rapidly explained) I would order my license from the Prefecture. I thanked him. I shook his hand, but he hardly expected the gesture and barely acknowledged it.

Then I got out, saying good-bye to M. Georges.

I waved the license at the girl, who smiled, then I headed down the avenue Maurice-Tardat, more or less in the direction of the center of town. In about ten minutes I realized that I would have to take a bus—it was much too far to walk home. In that same direction the overgrown boy had also headed, but he was no longer in sight.

For a long time after receiving my license, I never failed to wave at Claude and M. Georges whenever they drove by with their new students. I even went out of my way to wave. This at first surprised and then greatly displeased Françoise, who felt not only that I had suffered enough at their hands but also that I had been badly taught, especially whenever I shifted into fourth in town, drove at over 130 km/h (= 81 mph) on a wet tollway, or did not signal long enough in advance before turning.

"When I learned how to drive," Françoise would insist, "we were not expected to drive so recklessly!"

Nor was my case exceptional. Vincent, Cornelia, Frédéric, Élisabeth—many of our friends, in different schools, in different towns, confirmed that they too had gone through what I had gone through.

So why back then did I continue to wave at Claude and M. Georges, even long after they had forgotten who I was, when raising their hands haltingly above the windowsill they would scrutinize my face inquisitively?

I think I could tell you quite a lot about that waving . . . but what I know pains me and makes me afraid—of myself.

Angers 1988–1991

Biographical Note

John Taylor (b. 1952) is an American writer, critic, and translator who was born in Des Moines and has lived in France since 1977. He is the author of eleven volumes of short prose and poetry. His most recent titles include *The Dark Brightness* (Xenos Books), *Grassy Stairways* (The MadHat Press), *Remembrance of Water & Twenty-Five Trees* (The Bitter Oleander Press), and a "double book" co-authored with Pierre Chappuis, *A Notebook of Clouds & A Notebook of Ridges* (The Fortnightly Review). Many of his books have been translated into French, four into Italian, one into Serbian, while selected poems, stories, and essays have appeared in a dozen other languages. Taylor has also translated some of the key Modern Greek, Italian, and especially French poets. His essays on European literature have been gathered in five volumes by Transaction Publishers (now Routledge): *A Little Tour through European Poetry*, *Into the Heart of European Poetry*, and the three-volume *Paths to Contemporary French Literature*.

CPSIA information can be obtained
at www.ICGtesting.com
Printed in the USA
JSHW050711161020
8813JS00001B/2